Forgotten African Fairy Tales

Untold African Oral Narratives, Volume 1

Wasike

Published by Wasike, 2024.

FORGOTTEN AFRICAN FAIRY TALES

First edition. October 27, 2024.

ISBN: 979-8227082046

Written by Wasike.

Table of Contents

Nakitumba Saves Her Jealous Sisters...1

i). Nakitumba's unique Attributes..2

ii). Triumph at the Village Square...5

iii). Eleven Mysterious Men...8

iv). Nakitumba's Doubts the Eleven Men's Intention 11

v). Nakitumba's Overcomes Major Hurdles...13

vi). Uncovering Eleven Men's True Identity..15

vii). Nakitumba's Outsmarts the Giants 18

viii). Nakitumba Brings her Sisters Back Home 21

A Narrow Escape 23

i). Selah's Unique Endowment..24

ii). Pretense among Friends..26

iii). A Strange Old Woman and the Lost Necklace 29

iv). Selah's Disappearance 32

v). The Great Search...35

vi). Uncovering Selah's Whereabouts..38

Natela Learns Her Lesson the Hard Way 41

i). Contradicting Worldviews 42

ii). Esinas in the Wonderland...44

iii). The Price of Greed 46

Origin of Bukusu Knife (Embalu) 49

i). Mango's Birth and its Significance to Bukusu Culture......................50

ii). Preparation for Future Roles...52

iii). A Horrifying Invasion 54

iv). Panic in the Bukusu Land 56

v). Preparation for the Hunt...58

vi). The Great Hunt...60

vii). Mango's Relentless Determination 62

viii). An Encounter with Ekhilakhima..64

ix). A Strategic Plan to Neutralize the Serpent 66

x). The Final Blow..68

xi). Triumph in Bukusu Land..70

xii). Mango Receives the Cut...73

Kasawa and Liondo, the Mysterious Pumpkin Fruit 75

i). Kasawa's Mysterious Workplace 76

ii). Danger at Kasawa's Doorstep 77

iii). Disobedience and Death in Kasawa's Home 79

iv). The Mysterious White Pigeon 82

v). Disseminating the Message 84

vi). An Encounter with the Bukusu Sacred Land 87

vii). The Sacred Leaf and the Redemption of Bukusu Land 90

Gûkumbacwo in Muiruri's Farm 94

i).Gaturu the Lazy Squirrel 95

ii). Gaturu's Love for Free Things 97

iii). Confrontation in Muiruri's Farm 98

Naswa and the Talking Pumpkin Fruit 101

The Cry of the Widow's Son 104

Forgotten African Fairy Tales: Untold African Oral Narratives

By Caleb Mukono Wasike

Edition One

Author's Biography

C. M. Wasike is a renowned author and tutor from Western Kenya. He is the lastborn in the family of nine. The author holds a Bachelor of Arts Degree in African languages and literature from Kibabii University, Kenya.

Acknowledgement

I dedicate this book to the Almighty God, my esteemed parents for exposing me to significant amount of African literature during my childhood. I also thank my beautiful and wonderful daughters for the immense support when I was compiling this literature. May the Almightily God bless you.

Nakitumba Saves Her Jealous Sisters

i). Nakitumba's unique Attributes

In the lively village of Chebukaka, the air buzzed with excitement and anticipation. The village was preparing for a grand feast, a special occasion where many families gave their daughters' hands in marriage to young men from both the village and neighboring communities. The celebration promised a blend of joy, music, and dancing that would unite families and forge new bonds.

Three days ago, Elder Mukari, one of the respected elders of Chebukaka village, had been busy preparing his daughters for this big day. Mukari and his three wives had spent most of their treasured cowry shells purchasing beautiful outfits for eleven of his twelve daughters. The eleven girls, adorned in their new, vibrant dancing attire, twirled and danced around their home, admiring themselves and giggling with excitement.

But one daughter, Nakitumba, stood quietly aside, her heart heavy with a mix of longing and sadness. Unlike her sisters, she had no new clothes to try on and no excitement to share. Born with a hump on her back, Nakitumba was often excluded by her sisters. They whispered behind her back, saying she wasn't fit to join them in the celebrations because of her "unfortunate condition."

As her sisters danced and chatted about the upcoming feast, Nakitumba watched silently. She wished she could join them and feel the joy of the moment, but her sisters wouldn't let her. They would not allow her to speak about their beautiful dresses or share in their excitement. Feeling left out, Nakitumba tried to focus on other tasks, but deep down, she longed for acceptance and a chance to prove that she, too, could bring joy and value to her family and community.

Though her sisters treated her with disdain, Nakitumba's heart remained kind and gentle. She found comfort in her mother's words, who often told her, "You are special, my dear, not because of what you look like, but because of the goodness in your heart." However, on this day, as she watched her sisters whirl around in their bright, new outfits, Nakitumba wondered if she would ever get the chance to show her worth.

Nakitumba failed to understand that fate had a different plan for her. A moment was coming where she would have the opportunity to step out of the shadows and show everyone that true strength and beauty come from within.

Word spread quickly through the village of Chebukaka that eleven men from a neighboring community would be attending the feast. This news sent ripples of excitement among all the girls in the village. They eagerly whispered among themselves, wondering which of the men might choose them as a future bride. Their eyes sparkled with dreams of love and admiration, and the preparations became even livelier.

However, Nakitumba wasn't swept up in the excitement like her sisters and the other girls. While they danced and talked of the potential suitors, her mind was elsewhere. Instead of thinking about dresses or marriages, Nakitumba was busy feeding Nangila, a pet frog that lived in a small nook at the back of her family's kitchen. Nangila was more than just a pet to her—he was her companion, her confidant, and, in some ways, her best friend.

Nakitumba had a special gift, a unique ability that no one else seemed to notice except for her beautiful mother. She could communicate with animals of all kinds—frogs, birds, goats, even the shyest of forest creatures. She had a way of understanding them and making them feel safe. She would spend hours talking to them, singing softly, or just sitting quietly, listening to their small, silent stories.

On this day, while the village buzzed with anticipation, Nakitumba sat at the back of the kitchen, carefully catching grasshoppers. She knew Nangila loved them best. She placed each one delicately in front of him, smiling as his big, round eyes blinked with delight before he caught them in one quick flick of his tongue. "There you go, Nangila," she whispered, her voice soft and gentle. "Enjoy your feast, too."

As she watched Nangila eat, she felt a sense of peace. She didn't need fancy dresses or to be noticed by the visiting men. She felt content being who she was—a friend to the animals and someone who could see the beauty in all creatures, no matter how big or small.

Her mother would often tell her, "You have a heart that sees beyond what others see, my Nakitumba. That is a gift." Today, as Nakitumba spent time with her frog friend, she remembered her mother's words and smiled. She knew that while her sisters focused on the feast, she had a world of her own—one filled with creatures who loved her for exactly who she was.

Unknown to her, this gift of hers would soon become the key to saving the day for the entire village of Chebukaka.

ii). Triumph at the Village Square

The long-awaited day of the feast finally dawned, and excitement filled the air in the village of Chebukaka. Girls from every corner of the village, adorned in their most colorful dresses, flocked to the famous village square, the center where every major event took place. The square was alive with the rhythmic sounds of traditional instruments—the deep, resonant beats of the *isukuti* drums, the melodic tunes of the *lulwika* and *litungu,* the cheerful notes of the *siilili,* the jingling of *bichenche* bells, and the lively clatter of the *kumulele* and *vifwototo.* The music echoed through the hills and valleys, and even the crows seemed to join in, cawing loudly as if to announce the day's festivities.

While some of the community members were gathering at the square, others remained at home, busy preparing delicacies for their future in-laws and husbands. Elder Mukari's first wife, Khalayi, along with her co-wives Nandako and Nelima, stayed back to prepare *sifuluko,* a savory traditional dish meant to impress the guests from the neighboring community. Their kitchen bustled with activity as they stirred pots, ground spices, and arranged the food with care.

Nakitumba had also stayed at home, assisting her mother with various tasks. She chopped vegetables, fetched water, and carefully arranged the cooking stones. She found peace in the kitchen, away from the judging eyes of her sisters.

The previous night, her sisters, led by the eldest, Selah, had gathered around Nakitumba with stern faces. They warned her not to show her face at the party or in the visitors' room when they brought their potential husbands from the village square. "Don't you dare embarrass us, Nakitumba," Selah had said sharply. "Your looks... they're a disappointment. We don't want you to scare away our future husbands."

The words had cut deep, but Nakitumba swallowed her pain and focused on her chores. She had grown accustomed to their harsh words, yet each one still stung like a thorn. She knew they saw her hump as a curse, something that made her less valuable in their eyes.

But Nakitumba's mother, Nelima, noticed the sadness in her daughter's eyes. She placed a gentle hand on Nakitumba's shoulder and whispered, "My child, you are more beautiful than any of them can see. Do not let their words dim your light." Nakitumba nodded, her heart warmed by her mother's kindness, but deep down, she still longed for acceptance from her sisters.

As the sounds of music and celebration drifted into their home, Nakitumba continued to help with the preparations, pretending not to hear her sisters' laughter from the distance. She knew the feast was a time of joy and union, but for her, it felt like another reminder of where she did not belong.

Yet, in her heart, a small flicker of hope remained. She didn't know why, but something told her that this day would be different. While her sisters danced and dreamed of marriage, Nakitumba would soon have a chance to show that her worth was not defined by her appearance but by the strength of her spirit and the kindness in her heart.

As the community continued to enjoy the lively sounds of the music, a hush fell over the crowd. The reason for the sudden silence was the arrival of eleven handsome men, each riding a majestic white horse. The men looked regal, dressed in fine attire, their eyes scanning the festive gathering before them. The rhythmic beats of the drums and the melodies of the instruments stopped abruptly, and all attention turned to the newcomers.

The master of ceremonies, a tall, elderly man with a booming voice, stepped forward and raised his hand to quiet the crowd. "Welcome, welcome, esteemed guests from our neighboring community!" he announced warmly, his voice carrying across the square. "Please, take your seats and enjoy our hospitality."

As the men dismounted from their horses and took their seats, the music began again, this time even more vibrant and full of energy. The air was charged with excitement, and all the girls in the square couldn't help but steal glances at the eleven men. Even those who had already been betrothed to Chebukaka men couldn't resist casting their eyes toward the newcomers, drawn by their charm and the prospect of a fresh start.

The ceremony began in earnest, with different groups of girls eagerly taking to the stage, each trying to outshine the last with their dance moves. They swayed and twirled, their colorful dresses flowing like water, their anklets jingling with each step. The crowd cheered them on, clapping to the beat, but the excitement truly reached a fever pitch when Elder Mukari's daughters stepped forward.

The daughters of Elder Mukari were known throughout Chebukaka for their beauty and grace. But today, they had outdone themselves. Dressed in vibrant, eye-catching attire that sparkled in the sunlight, they moved as one, their bodies swaying and twisting with a rhythm that seemed almost magical. Their dance was not only graceful but filled with complex footwork and elegant hand movements, captivating everyone present.

Suddenly, they stole the show. The entire crowd erupted into cheers, their applause louder than it had been for any of the previous groups. The energy was electric, and the music seemed to pulse even harder as if matching the heartbeat of the excited crowd. The eleven men, clearly impressed, stood up from their seats and walked into the dancing space.

With broad smiles and looks of admiration, the men began to spray the dancing daughters with cowry shells, a sign of appreciation, admiration, and, possibly, a proposal. Shells rained down on the girls, bouncing off their shimmering outfits and landing on the ground like precious pearls. The daughters' eyes sparkled with pride and delight; their hard work and preparations had paid off.

This was not the case with the previous dance groups. The men had remained seated, merely clapping politely. But Elder Mukari's daughters had brought them to their feet. As the music played on, louder and faster, the girls danced with even more vigor, their spirits lifted by the attention they were receiving. Nakitumba, although she was at home, the cheers from the village square melted here hears. Although she paid little attention to it, she wished she could be there to watch her sisters' dances.

iii). Eleven Mysterious Men

That evening, Elder Mukari's daughters returned from the village square, their faces glowing with happiness and pride. The eleven men, who had been thoroughly impressed by the daughters' performance, had followed them back to their father's compound. Their intention was clear: they had come to ask for the daughters' hands in marriage. According to the customs of Bukusu people, this was a highly significant moment, marking the beginning of new family ties.

As tradition dictated, Elder Mukari's potential sons-in-law were to be served a delicious traditional meal, prepared with great care, to honor them and solidify their intentions. The meal was a grand affair, meant to impress and show the hospitality and generosity of the host family. The kitchen was filled with the tantalizing aroma of freshly cooked sifuluko, a delicacy made from fermented millet and fish, along with other sumptuous dishes that made one's mouth water.

However, before the eleven daughters began serving their visitors, they sternly warned Nakitumba to stay in her room. "Do not show your face in the dining room!" they hissed at her, their voices sharp and filled with disdain. They feared that her presence, with her humpback and simple demeanor, would ruin their chance to impress the handsome visitors.

Resigned to her fate, Nakitumba remained in her small room, her heart heavy. She could hear the clatter of dishes and the hum of polite conversation from the dining room. Elder Mukari and the elders were seated outside, discussing how they would conduct the short ceremony that was to follow the meal. Inside the kitchen, Khalayi and her co-wives, Nandako and Nelima, were chatting with the daughters, giving them last-minute advice on marital issues and how to behave as new brides.

Meanwhile, in her room, Nakitumba tried to distract herself from the festivities and her exclusion. But then, she heard a strange murmur coming from the dining room, as if the visitors were unhappy about something. Curiosity got the better of her, and she carefully crept to the door, peeking through a small crack.

To her horror, she saw one of the visitors—the one who had been sitting at the head of the table—remove an entire plate of *sifuluko* from his mouth. His jaws seemed to have unhinged like a snake's, and he devoured the food with such unnatural ease that it sent chills down Nakitumba's spine. The plate itself seemed to vanish into his mouth, swallowed whole, as if it had never existed. His eyes were vacant, almost hollow, with a faint, eerie glow to them.

The other visitors were not far behind; their behavior grew more bizarre with each passing moment. Some of them were eating the food without using their hands, their mouths stretching to impossible sizes. Others had begun to gnaw on the wooden plates themselves, their sharp teeth leaving deep grooves in the once-smooth surfaces.

Nakitumba's heart raced as she realized what was happening. The visitors who had come to ask for her sisters' hands in marriage were not human. They were *manan*i—ancient giants from the forbidden mountains, known for their ability to shape-shift and impersonate humans. Legends said they fed on human flesh and could disguise themselves as charming men or women to lure unsuspecting victims.

The realization sent a shiver down her spine. She knew she had to do something. Her sisters and the entire family were in grave danger, and the *manani* were likely planning to devour them once they had dropped their guard. But how could she warn everyone without revealing herself and risking being seen as a fool? She knew no one would believe her—her sisters had always dismissed her as nothing more than a burden.

Still, she couldn't let fear paralyze her. She had to act, and she had to act fast. With a deep breath, Nakitumba decided to call upon the only creatures who might listen to her—the animals. She quickly slipped out the back door and whispered to Nangila, her frog pet, to spread the word among the animals of the village. If they could create a distraction, she might have a chance to expose the *manani* and save her family.

WASIKE

Her heart pounding, Nakitumba hoped that her bond with the animals would be enough to save the day. She could only pray that they would come to her aid in time, before the *manani* revealed their true, monstrous nature.

iv). Nakitumba's Doubts the Eleven Men's Intention

After the meal, the eleven men excused themselves and stepped outside to meet with the elders for a brief ceremony. The elders, led by Elder Mukari, sat under the large sycamore tree in front of the house. Their faces appeared stern and dignified, eager to know more about his potential son in-laws. The elders asked them to share about their homes, lineage, and other critical details that could help identify them and establish their place in the community. The men spoke confidently, spinning tales of grand homes and wealthy families from neighboring communities, giving names of clans that were known to the elders.

The elders, satisfied with the answers, nodded approvingly. None of them suspected that the charming men before them were anything but what they appeared to be. Every detail sounded plausible, every story was convincing. Elder Mukari even smiled, his eyes crinkling with satisfaction at the thought of having such fine men as sons-in-law. Yet, everything the men said was a lie, and the *manani* had perfected the art of deception over centuries.

Meanwhile, inside the house, Nakitumba paced back and forth, her mind racing with fear and frustration. She knew she had to act quickly. With the elders and her sisters enchanted by these false men, she had to find a way to expose the truth. Summoning her courage, Nakitumba sneaked out of her room and rushed to the kitchen, where her sisters were giddy with excitement, preparing themselves for the marriage ceremony.

"Nasambu!" Nakitumba whispered urgently, her voice trembling. "You must listen to me. These men are not who they claim to be! I saw them—one swallowed an entire plate, and another was chewing on the wooden plate itself. They are *manani*, ancient giants who have come to deceive us. They are not human!"

Her sisters turned to her, eyes widening with surprise. But their surprise quickly turned to scorn and laughter. "Oh, Nakitumba," scoffed Selah, the eldest sister. "Stop these wild stories! Are you jealous that we are finally getting married and you are not? Stop trying to ruin our day with your nonsense."

Another sister, Nanjakho, chimed in, "Yes, you always have these strange ideas in your head. You've been talking to that silly frog of yours too much! Go back to your room and stay out of this." Nakitumba felt a surge of desperation. She tried to grab Sella's arm, her eyes pleading. "Please, I beg you! Believe me, just this once. This is not about jealousy. They will eat us all if we don't act now!"

But before she could say another word, her sisters, irritated by what they perceived as another one of her 'antics,' seized her by her arms. Taking advantage of her weight and her helplessness, they lifted her up, dragging her back to her room. "Stay there and keep your crazy thoughts to yourself," they scolded, closing the door firmly behind her.

Nakitumba banged on the door, but it was no use. Her sisters were convinced she was simply envious and trying to sabotage their chance at happiness. She knew she had to warn Elder Mukari, but she could hear the music picking up again outside and knew she was running out of time. From her small window, she could see the elders, including her father, nodding and laughing as they conversed with the men. The fake suitors had charmed everyone.

The elders, led by Elder Mukari, called the girls outside for a short marriage ceremony. Nakitumba's sisters, dressed in their finest, paraded out of the house with their heads held high, leaving Nakitumba helplessly behind. The brief ceremony involved a simple exchange of cowry shells and blessings from the elders, symbolizing the betrothal. It was all happening too fast, and Nakitumba felt a knot tighten in her chest.

As the ceremony concluded, everyone prepared to return to the village square for more dancing and celebration, unaware of the danger that loomed. The sounds of drums, flutes, and singing filled the air again, and the crowd began moving towards the square. The dance would go on until midnight, and for Nakitumba, every minute that passed felt like a step closer to disaster. Trapped in her room, Nakitumba knew she couldn't give up. She would have to think of another way to save her family before it was too late.

v). Nakitumba's Overcomes Major Hurdles

Nakitumba's loyal pet, Nangila, had been watching closely all day. The small frog knew his friend needed help, and when he hopped over to his dear friend, Ekhima the Monkey, he quickly shared the troubling news of how Nakitumba had been locked away in her room. Ekhima, a clever and agile monkey known for his daring escapades, understood the urgency. "We have to get her out, Nangila," he said, his eyes narrowing with determination.

As night fell, Nangila the frog and Ekhima the Monkey crept silently to Nakitumba's window, careful not to alert anyone inside the house. Ekhima skillfully climbed the wall, using his tiny yet strong hands to loosen the wooden bars that held the window shut. Once the window was pried open, Nangila croaked softly to signal Nakitumba. She peeked through the darkness, her heart lifting when she saw her two friends. With Ekhima's help, she carefully climbed out of the window, her feet landing softly on the ground outside.

"Thank you, my friends," she whispered, her voice filled with gratitude. "I must go to the village square and save my sisters before it's too late."

With a sense of urgency, Nakitumba ran towards the village square, where the celebrations were still ongoing, music and laughter echoing into the night. She needed a plan. She hid near the area where the eleven men had tied their white horses and tried to think of the best remedy to expose the truth. As she crouched behind a large bush, her mind raced through possible ideas.

Suddenly, she remembered her friend, Wanami, the clever and strong baboon who lived in a hidden cave nearby. Wanami was known for his sharp instincts and bravery. Without wasting another moment, Nakitumba let out three short, distinct whistles, a secret signal known only to her animal friends. The night seemed to hold its breath for a moment, and then, from the shadows of the trees, Wanami appeared, swinging down with ease.

"What brings you here, Nakitumba?" Wanami asked, his deep voice rumbling softly.

Quickly, Nakitumba explained the entire situation—the strange behavior of the eleven men, how she had been locked away, and the need to save her sisters from becoming victims of the *manani*. Wanami listened intently, his eyes narrowing with concern. "These are dangerous beings," he said, "but we will follow them and find out where they are taking your sisters."

As they planned their next move, the eleven men returned to their horses with Elder Mukari's daughters, ready to leave. The girls, still enchanted by the charm of these seemingly handsome men, climbed up on the horses' backs, unaware of the danger. The eleven men began their journey, taking their new brides away from the village square under the cover of darkness.

Nakitumba, determined and fearless, decided to follow them. She climbed onto Wanami's strong back, and the two friends stealthily moved after the group. Thanks to Wanami's agility, they stayed hidden among the tree tops, leaping silently from branch to branch. None of the eleven men or the girls noticed them, as they were too focused on their journey ahead.

From above, Nakitumba watched carefully. She noticed the strange way the men moved, and how they seemed to communicate with each other in hushed, unfamiliar tones. She could also see how the moonlight made their features seem distorted and less human. Her heart pounded in her chest, knowing she had to act fast. With every leap, she and Wanami were getting closer to uncovering the truth and finding a way to save her sisters from these ancient giants.

vi). Uncovering Eleven Men's True Identity

At daybreak, the eleven men led Nakitumba's sisters to a massive building with towering walls and a roof that seemed to stretch up to the sky. The structure was unlike anything the girls had ever seen, with its tall wooden beams and strange symbols carved into the walls. Inside, the air felt thick and heavy, as if it carried an ancient secret. Nakitumba, who had managed to stay hidden during the journey, appeared at the doorway just as her sisters were ushered in.

Her sisters were startled to see her there. "What are you doing here, Nakitumba?" they hissed, trying to push her out. But they were far from home now, and their usual tactics to eject her didn't work. One of the eleven men, who appeared to be the leader, noticed the commotion and approached them with a smile that didn't quite reach his eyes. "Leave her be," he said in a strangely soothing tone. "Our home is large enough for all. She may stay with you."

Over the next five days, the eleven girls were treated like queens. They were given the finest clothes, delicious meals, and soft beds to sleep on. They were pampered with luxurious baths, exotic perfumes, and jewelry that shimmered in the sunlight. The men seemed to dote on them endlessly, always smiling, always kind. To the unsuspecting sisters, it felt like they were living in a dream. But Nakitumba, always the observer, stayed cautious. She watched every move their hosts made, her sharp eyes never missing a detail. She noticed how, despite the men's kindness, their eyes would sometimes flash with something dark and unnatural. She saw how they never ate with the girls, only watching them intently during meals. She knew something was not right.

On the sixth day, as the sun began to set and shadows crept across the floor of the grand building, Nakitumba overheard a conversation that sent chills down her spine. She had hidden herself behind a thick curtain when she heard one of the men speaking in a low, urgent voice. "The dose that turned us into humans will expire tonight," he whispered, his voice filled with a mix of anxiety and anticipation.

The others nodded in agreement. "Yes," another replied, "we must prepare a grand feast for our guests tonight. They must be fed well, fattened for the... occasion."

Nakitumba's heart pounded in her chest as she realized the gravity of the situation. The men weren't human at all—they were *manani,* ancient giants who had only disguised themselves to lure the girls away. And now, with their true forms about to be revealed, they planned to turn her sisters into a feast!

She knew she had little time to act. She had to think quickly and find a way to save her sisters from this deadly trap. Keeping calm, she carefully backed away from the curtain and hurried to find Wanami, her baboon friend, who had stayed nearby. She needed a plan, and she needed it fast. The lives of her sisters depended on her next move.

That night, Nakitumba lay awake, her body tense and her eyes fixed on the shadows dancing across the walls. Her sisters slept soundly beside her, snoring in blissful ignorance. She had heard enough to know that something terrible was going to happen. She couldn't let her guard down for even a moment. As the village clock struck midnight, she noticed movement from the corner of her eye. The eleven men were rising from their beds, their faces drawn with a strange intensity. One by one, they signaled to each other and moved silently toward the main room of the massive house.

Nakitumba slipped out of bed, her feet barely making a sound on the cool floor. She tiptoed after them, keeping to the shadows. When she reached the main room, she hid behind a large wooden pillar, her breath held tight. The eleven men huddled together, speaking in hushed tones. She strained her ears to hear their conversation, her heart pounding in her chest.

"We must prepare for the transformation," whispered one of the men, his voice low and gravelly. "The pain is worth it if it means we can feed on their flesh once we return to our true forms."

Nakitumba's eyes widened as she continued to listen. They spoke of how they had overheard villagers talking about the upcoming feast in Chebukaka and became determined to attend. But as giants—*manani*—they needed a way to disguise themselves as humans. They sought out an old medicine man known for his dark and mysterious magic. The old man had instructed them to find an anthill and place their tongues into it, allowing the ants to bite them repeatedly. "The pain," one of the giants muttered, his face contorting with the memory, "was excruciating. We did it for seven days straight."

On the seventh day, the medicine man provided them with a concoction of Bukusu traditional herbs that, when taken, would complete their transformation into men. Nakitumba's stomach churned as she imagined the grotesque process.

The most chilling revelation was that out of sheer greed and arrogance, the giants had decided to devour the old medicine man before they could learn about the exact herb or its antidote that would allow them to transform back into humans at will. "Fools," muttered another, "we killed the only one who could have given us the knowledge to maintain the transformation. Now, we must wait until the dose wears off."

vii). Nakitumba's Outsmarts the Giants

Nakitumba felt a cold shiver run down her spine. The men's transformation was temporary, and once they reverted to their true forms, they planned to feast on her sisters. They were trapped in a predicament of their own making—human by day and waiting to revert to monstrous giants by nightfall.

Realizing the urgency of the situation, Nakitumba knew she needed to act immediately. She couldn't allow these monstrous beings to harm her sisters. But she also knew that she had to be smart about it. She tiptoed back to the room, carefully avoiding any sound, and woke Wanami, her baboon friend, who was sleeping by the window. Whispering softly, she told him everything she had heard and together they quickly began to devise a plan. Nakitumba needed to find a way to trick the giants into revealing their true selves before they could harm anyone. She would need courage, wit, and a bit of luck to outsmart the *manani*. Time was running out, and the fate of her sisters depended on her next move.

After sneaking back to her bed, Nakitumba lay still, her mind racing with the information she had gathered. The room was eerily quiet, but she could sense the impending danger as the giants prepared for their nefarious plans. She watched with bated breath as one of the giants began to transform, his jaw elongating grotesquely and glowing with a menacing red light. Nakitumba's heart pounded, but she forced herself to remain calm.

With a quick, decisive move, she let out a soft groan and moaned, "Mmmmmh! kindly take me out to ease myself." Her voice was laced with urgency. The giant, momentarily taken aback, reverted to his human form and offered to escort her to the toilet, wary of making any suspicious moves.

As they walked outside, Nakitumba's mind was already working on her next strategy. Once they reached the toilet, she pretended to struggle, buying herself some time to think. After a few moments, she thanked the giant and returned to the house, her thoughts racing with possible solutions.

Upon re-entering, she saw the men start to transform back into their monstrous forms, their grotesque features emerging in the dim light. Before they could cause any harm, Nakitumba seized the opportunity. She pretended to wake up, feigning a need for water. "I only drink water from *Musebele*," she declared loudly. "And it must be fetched using a sieve."

The giants, desperate to keep their secret and avoid raising suspicion, grudgingly agreed to fetch water for her, even though they were visibly irritated. They took several sieves and made their way to the nearby spring, grumbling and muttering as they went.

Once they were gone, Nakitumba swiftly woke her sisters. She recounted everything she had overheard and witnessed, her voice trembling with urgency. At first, her sisters were skeptical, but her elder sister, who had been observing closely since their arrival, believed her. She was convinced by the evidence and took Nakitumba's warnings seriously.

Quickly, the sisters rallied together, gathering their belongings and preparing for their escape. They moved quietly through the house, avoiding any noise that might alert the giants. With Nakitumba leading the way, they made their way through the dark corridors and out into the open.

The spring was several kilometers south of the giants' lair, and the girls, led by Nakitumba, moved swiftly through the dense forest under the faint glow of the moon. Nakitumba's heart pounded as she navigated her sisters away from danger, relying on the shadows of the night to conceal their escape. They crept through the cold woods, unsure of their path. Every step was a challenge—tree stumps tripped them, and thorns scratched their legs. The forest was eerily silent; no animals could be seen, for the giants had devoured them all before their transformation into men.

Suddenly, the twelve sisters reached the banks of a wide river with no boat or raft in sight. Panic set in as they began to argue, blaming one another for not heeding Nakitumba's warnings. As the tension rose, Nakitumba stepped carefully into the river and whispered softly. In an instant, a giant frog named Namakanda emerged from the water, towering over them. The sheer size of the creature terrified the eleven sisters, but Nakitumba remained calm. She spoke to Namakanda in a secret language only she understood, and soon the frog agreed to help. It explained that the only way to cross the river was for it to swallow them whole and swim them across to safety. With no other options, the sisters reluctantly agreed. One by one, Namakanda swallowed them, finishing with a mouthful of clay from the riverbank. After a few moments of rest, the frog dove into the river, beginning the long swim home.

viii). Nakitumba Brings her Sisters Back Home

Meanwhile, the giants were still at the spring, futilely trying to fetch water with their sieves. Each time, the water drained away until one of them had the idea to smear clay over the holes to hold the water. With this trick, they managed to fill the sieves and started back to the house. When they arrived, darkness still shrouded everything, making it hard to see clearly.

"Nakitumba!" a giant thundered. "Eeh!" a soft voice answered from under a bed. "Where are you?" the giant demanded. "I am under the bed," the voice responded. "Get your water, you foolish girl!" growled the giant. But it was a clever trick—Nakitumba had trained a praying mantis to mimic her voice and distract the giants. The praying mantis darted around the room, keeping the giants occupied until dawn. When they realized they had been deceived, the giants scattered in all directions, desperately searching for the twelve girls. Eventually, they stumbled upon Namakanda resting by the riverbank.

"Did you see anyone cross the river?" one of the giants asked. Namakanda shook its head. "Why is your belly so large today? What have you eaten?" another giant questioned. "Only my usual meals," the frog replied. They ordered it to spit, and out came clumps of clay. Satisfied, the giants continued their fruitless search, allowing Namakanda to slip back into the river and swim toward Chebukaka village.

Inside Namakanda's belly, the journey felt endless. The sisters clung to each other in the dark, their hearts racing. Nakitumba, however, remained composed, whispering reassurances to calm them. She knew that fear would only make things worse. Finally, Namakanda reached the other side and crawled onto the riverbank, tired but determined.

The frog hopped slowly toward Elder Mukari's compound, where Khalayi and her friend Nekoye were deep in conversation about the recent festival. "I'm happy that all eleven of my beautiful daughters found favor in the eyes of such handsome young men," said Khalayi. The women's chatter abruptly stopped as Namakanda emerged from the bushes. The frog asked Nakitumba's mother for a warm bath, promising a special gift in return. Ever wise and gracious, Khalayi agreed. After the bath, Namakanda, now clean and relaxed, opened its massive mouth and out came the twelve girls, one after another.

The entire village soon gathered at Elder Mukari's home, astonished by the incredible sight. Overwhelmed with joy, Elder Mukari embraced his daughters, who tearfully confessed their foolishness in ignoring Nakitumba's warnings. They recounted their harrowing ordeal, and Mukari immediately ordered his warriors to set traps around the forest and river to eliminate any remaining threats. By the next day, the warriors had successfully neutralized all eleven giants.

In the midst of the celebrations, Elder Mukari summoned the villagers and honored his brave daughter. "Nakitumba has shown us that true beauty lies not in appearance but in courage, wisdom, and kindness," he declared. The villagers cheered, and her sisters, filled with remorse, apologized to her, vowing never to judge anyone by their looks again. That day, Nakitumba became the celebrated hero of Chebukaka village, her story of courage spreading far and wide.

The feast that followed was even more spectacular than the original event, with the village celebrating both the safety of the girls and Nakitumba's bravery. And so, the legend of Nakitumba's courage lived on, inspiring generations to come.

The End

A Narrow Escape

i). Selah's Unique Endowment

In the village of Wesakulila, nestled among rolling hills and lush green fields, lived a girl named Selah. From the moment she was born, it was clear that she possessed a rare beauty. As she grew, her beauty only blossomed further, captivating the eyes and hearts of everyone in the community. Her long, flowing hair glistened like the morning sun, her eyes sparkled like the night stars, and her smile was like a gentle breeze that brought comfort to all who saw it.

Selah's charm, however, went beyond her physical appearance. Raised by her loving parents, Elder Mukari and his wife, Khalayi, she had been taught the values of kindness, humility, and grace. She was not only beautiful on the outside but also possessed a heart filled with compassion. Her presence alone could light up a room, and her laughter was like music that soothed the soul. She greeted everyone she met with a warm smile and treated everyone with respect, regardless of their status or age.

Elder Mukari and Khalayi adored their daughter. They saw in her a rare combination of beauty and goodness, a blessing they were grateful for every day. At night, they would sit outside their mud-thatched house under the vast, starry sky and pray together. "May our Selah find a good man to marry," Khalayi would whisper, her hands clasped tightly together. "One who sees her heart and cherishes her for who she is."

Out of this deep love, Khalayi had given Selah a valuable necklace that she herself had been gifted by her mother before her demise nine years ago. The necklace was made of intricately woven gold, with a single, radiant gemstone at its center that shimmered in the sunlight. To Khalayi, the necklace was more than just a piece of jewelry; it was a symbol of her mother's love, wisdom, and the strength of the women in their family. On a quiet evening, she had tied it gently around Selah's neck, her eyes misty with emotion.

"Wear this always, my daughter," Khalayi had said softly, her voice trembling with both love and caution. "This necklace carries the spirit of your grandmother. It will protect you and guide you, but you must never take it off." Selah had nodded, understanding the gravity of her mother's words, and promised never to remove the necklace.

But in the midst of this admiration, Selah's beauty also stirred up a storm of jealousy among her peers. Many young men in the village dreamed of making her their wife, which made other young women feel overshadowed. This envy soon turned into bitterness and hatred. Instead of seeing her as a friend, they began to see her as competition.

Selah's friends would often gather under the big baobab tree near the river, where they would whisper behind her back. "She thinks she's better than us because of her looks," one would say, her voice dripping with disdain. "If only something would happen to her, maybe the men would notice us instead," another would add, her eyes narrowing with a mixture of envy and resentment. They would exchange glances filled with malice, wishing for something to tarnish her perfect image.

Unaware of the storm brewing around her, the girl continued her days with her usual grace, always believing in the goodness of those around her. She would often invite her friends to her home, offering fruits from her family's farm and sharing in their laughter. She believed that their smiles were genuine and that their friendship was as true as hers. Selah did not know that her friends' smiles concealed jealousy and spite.

Selah's spirit remained untarnished by the envy that surrounded her. She continued to shine brightly in the village of Wesakulila, with her mother's precious necklace always around her neck—a constant reminder of her family's love and the protection it promised.

But soon, the true depth of her friends' jealousy would be revealed, and Selah would find herself facing challenges she never could have imagined. The necklace, with its deep family roots, would come to play a crucial role in her fate, testing not only her resilience but also the strength of the love that had been passed down to her.

ii). Pretense among Friends

One morning, as the first rays of sunlight pierced through the morning mist, Selah's friends—Nasambu, Nekoye, Khakasa, and Nanjala—came to her home. They were on their way to fetch water from the spring, about a kilometer away, and wanted Selah to join them. It was a daily routine they enjoyed together, a time filled with chatter, laughter, and the simple pleasures of friendship.

As they walked down the well-trodden path, their laughter echoed through the still air. Soon, they were joined by five other girls, including Nandako, who harbored a secret dislike for Selah. She was envious of the attention Selah always seemed to receive, and her resentment had grown over time.

The journey to the spring was filled with fun stories and shared memories. The girls joked and teased one another, creating a sense of camaraderie that was both comforting and joyful. The morning sun rose higher, and the path became brighter, lined with wildflowers and the soft rustling of leaves in the gentle breeze.

Their lighthearted conversation was interrupted when they encountered three boys—Elima, Wafula, and Mukhebi—standing under a large acacia tree. The boys had been trying to win Selah's favor for some time, but their efforts had been in vain. As soon as they saw the group of girls approaching, their faces lit up. They greeted all the girls with enthusiasm, but it was clear that their attention was focused solely on Selah.

"Selah, could we have a word with you?" Elima asked, his voice tinged with both hope and nervousness.

Selah, ever polite and gentle, nodded. "Of course," she said, turning to her friends. "Please, give me a moment." The girls stepped aside, giving Selah some privacy to speak with the boys.

As they waited, Selah calmly explained to Elima, Wafula, and Mukhebi why she had turned down their advances before. "I am not ready to engage in any relationship," she said sincerely. "When the time is right, I will know, and so will the one meant for me."

While Selah spoke with the boys, Nandako's jealousy began to flare up. She watched the way the boys looked at Selah, with admiration and longing, and it fueled the bitterness that had been simmering in her heart. "Look at her," she muttered under her breath. "She's always turning down these boys, making them waste their time on her. Meanwhile, we are here, unnoticed because of her."

Nasambu, who was one of Selah's true friends, could not stand the unfair criticism. "Selah has the right to choose whom she wants to be with, just like any of us," she said firmly. "It's not her fault the boys are interested in her."

But Nandako's fury only grew. She clenched her fists and snapped, "And what about us? Why don't they see us? It's because she's always standing in their way, acting all virtuous!"

Without waiting for a response, Nandako stomped off, her face flushed with anger. She hurried ahead to the spring, muttering under her breath, her steps heavy with frustration. Reaching the spring first, she filled her pot with water quickly and stormed back up the path, ignoring the rest of the group.

Selah, having finished her conversation with the boys, rejoined her friends, her expression serene as always. She sensed the tension but chose not to dwell on it. With a warm smile, she gathered her remaining friends, and together they continued their walk to the spring.

The atmosphere was a bit strained, but Selah's presence always had a way of calming everyone. As they reached the cool, bubbling spring, she noticed Nandako already on her way back, her face set in a scowl. Selah felt a pang of concern but decided to let it pass. She dipped her gourd into the spring, the water cool against her hands, and smiled gently at her friends.

"Let's not worry about anything today," she said softly. "Let's just enjoy the beauty of the morning and the gift of each other's company."

Her words were simple but sincere, a reminder of the peace and simplicity they could all enjoy—if only they could let go of their jealousy and embrace genuine friendship. But for Nandako and some others, that peace was still a far way off, and their true feelings towards Selah would soon unfold in ways that no one could have predicted.

iii). A Strange Old Woman and the Lost Necklace

On arriving at the spring, Selah noticed a strange old woman sitting on the left side of the water source. The woman had an empty pot beside her and a drum-like container, both worn with age. Her presence was unusual, and the other girls seemed to avert their eyes, but Selah, ever respectful and kind, greeted the old woman with a polite nod and a warm smile.

"Good morning, Grandmother," Selah said softly. The old woman looked up slowly, her eyes clouded with age but sharp with awareness. She nodded in acknowledgment but said nothing, her expression unreadable. Selah felt a slight chill run down her spine but dismissed it, believing it was just the morning air.

The spring was unusually calm that day. Unlike the previous mornings, there were no long queues of women waiting to fetch water. The girls were relieved. They quickly filled their pots, the water cool and refreshing as it splashed against the earthenware. They laughed and joked as they worked, their earlier tension seemingly forgotten.

With their pots full, they began their journey back home. The morning sun had climbed higher, casting a golden glow over the landscape. They had barely gone far when Selah suddenly stopped. Her hand instinctively reached for her neck, and a wave of panic washed over her. Her valuable necklace—the one given to her by her mother, which she had promised never to remove—was missing.

"My necklace!" Selah exclaimed, her voice trembling. Her friends turned to look at her, some with genuine concern, while others barely hid their indifference. "It's gone. I must have dropped it at the spring."

She looked pleadingly at her friends. "Please, can you help me search for it? Or wait for me here while I go back to look for it?"

Nasambu, who had always been a true friend to Selah, nodded. "We'll wait here, Selah. Go and find it quickly."

But Nandako and the others exchanged sly glances. "Yes, we'll wait," Nandako said with a smile that didn't quite reach her eyes.

Selah, trusting her friends, hurried back to the spring, her heart pounding with anxiety. She couldn't bear the thought of losing the necklace, not just because of its value but because of what it meant—a connection to her mother and her late grandmother. As she approached the spring, she saw the old woman still sitting in the same place, her eyes following Selah's every move.

Selah knelt by the water's edge, her hands shaking as she searched the ground for the necklace. She combed through the grass and pebbles, her eyes scanning every inch. The sun's reflection on the water seemed to mock her, its brightness contrasting with the darkness of her growing despair. She was about to ask the old woman if she had seen the necklace when she noticed a slight movement from the corner of her eye. The old woman smiled—a knowing, almost eerie smile.

"Are you looking for something, child?" the old woman finally spoke, her voice raspy but calm.

Selah hesitated but nodded. "Yes grandmother. I lost my necklace. It's very important to me. Have you seen it?"

The old woman's smile deepened, and she slowly shook her head. "No, I haven't seen it. But be careful whom you trust, young one. Not all smiles are kind, and not all friends are true."

Selah felt a shiver down her spine again. The old woman's words seemed to carry a hidden weight, a truth that was beginning to dawn on her.

Meanwhile, back on the path, Nandako and the other girls had no intention of waiting for Selah. As soon as she was out of sight, they hurried back towards the village, snickering amongst themselves.

"Can you believe her?" Nandako sneered. "She acts so perfect, but now she's probably run off with some boy."

By the time they reached Selah's home, they had crafted a lie that would shake the trust Selah's parents had in her. Nandako, ever the outspoken one, rushed forward to speak with Khalayi, Selah's mother, who was tending to the goats near their compound.

"Auntie Khalayi," Nandako began, feigning breathlessness and concern, "we waited for Selah, but she didn't come back. We saw her heading off with a boy towards his house."

Khalayi's heart sank, but she remained calm. "Which boy?" she asked, her eyes narrowing as she studied Nandako's face.

Nandako shrugged. "We didn't see clearly, but we thought you should know. She's not where she's supposed to be."

Elder Mukari, Selah's father, overheard the conversation and frowned deeply. "What kind of behavior is this?" he muttered his voice stern and filled with disappointment. "Has she lost her sense?"

But Khalayi's heart, a mother's heart, was filled with doubt. She knew her daughter better than anyone. Selah was honest and respectful. Something about Nandako's story didn't sit right with her. She had always trusted her daughter deeply, and she could not shake the feeling that there was more to this than what Nandako was saying.

"Let us wait for Selah to come back and hear what she has to say," Khalayi said firmly, trying to hide her worry. She prayed silently that her daughter was safe and that this was all a misunderstanding.

Meanwhile, back at the spring, Selah continued her search. She felt tears pricking at her eyes as she realized the necklace might be lost forever. But the old woman's words echoed in her mind: "Not all friends are true." Was this a hint? Was someone behind the loss of her precious necklace?

The journey back home would not only be about finding the lost necklace but also about uncovering a painful truth about those she once called friends.

iv). Selah's Disappearance

Back at the spring, Selah saw the strange old woman filling her pot with water. The woman moved slowly, her frail hands carefully guiding the flow into the vessel. As soon as she noticed Selah approaching, the old woman looked up, her eyes glinting with an eerie familiarity.

"Are you still searching for your necklace, child?" the old woman asked in a raspy voice. Selah nodded, her heart pounding with hope and fear.

The old woman's wrinkled face softened into a smile. "Do not worry," she said, "I found it in the water. It's safe with me." Selah felt a wave of relief wash over her. The necklace, her most cherished possession, was not lost after all.

"But first," the old woman continued, her tone almost commanding, "help me fill my pot with water and rub my back. My old bones are weary."

Selah, ever kind and respectful, agreed. She filled the old woman's pot to the brim, the cool water splashing against her hands. Once the pot was full, the old woman gestured towards the lower section of the spring. "Come with me, child," she said, "I need to bathe, and I'll need your help."

Selah hesitated but felt obligated to assist. She followed the old woman to a more secluded part of the spring, where the woman began to undress. Selah averted her eyes out of respect, but she could feel the old woman's gaze on her. After she had undressed, the woman entered the water and sat down, her back towards Selah.

"Rub my back," the old woman instructed. Selah, her hands trembling slightly did as she was told. The old woman sighed in satisfaction as Selah's gentle hands eased the tension from her muscles. When she was finished, the woman stood up and slowly dressed herself. They returned to the old woman's original sitting spot, where the drum-like container still sat.

"Now, child," the old woman said, her voice taking on a mysterious tone, "your necklace is in that small container beside me. Go on, get it."

Selah, filled with anticipation, knelt down and reached for the container. Just as her fingers brushed the lid, the old woman's expression changed. Before Selah could react, the woman shoved her into the container with a surprising strength, slamming the lid shut. Selah's cries were muffled as darkness enveloped her.

In an instant, the old woman began to change. Her frail body grew larger, her skin toughening and darkening, her eyes glowing with a sinister light. The kind old woman was gone, replaced by a terrifying *Linani*—an ogre of immense size and power. The creature's voice boomed through the container, its tone menacing and cruel.

"Listen to me, girl," the *Linani* growled, its breath hot and foul. "If you misbehave, I will eat you alive! But if you do as I say, you may survive this ordeal."

Selah's heart raced with fear. She tried to cry out, but the container was too small and stifling, her voice barely a whisper in the tight space.

The *Linani* tapped the container three times with a heavy hand, causing it to rattle. "When I knock three times, you must entertain me with a song. If you fail, I will devour you!"

With that, the *Linani* began the ritual chant, its voice reverberating through the container:

Sili muno ni shi?

Sili muno ni shi?

Selah, trembling with terror, responded with a song, her voice shaky but melodious:

Nalekha esimbi yange Mumwalo

Nalekha esimbi yange Mumwalo

Bachi Njakhucheka kwenye machi kwikhale

Bachi Njakhucheka kwenye machi kwikhale

Linani, now satisfied, chuckled with dark delight. It had found a way to entertain itself while enjoying the local brew in the village, all without paying a single coin. The creature's malevolent plan was already taking shape in its twisted mind.

The ogre then transformed into the guise of an old man, hunching over as it made its way to Namalwa's joint—a popular spot in the village for local brew. Upon arriving, the old man struck a deal with Namalwa, promising to entertain her customers in exchange for several gourds of the finest local beer. That evening, Namalwa's business thrived like never before. The patrons were mesmerized by the old man's performances, unaware that the beautiful songs they were hearing were sung by the trapped and terrified Selah, confined within the small container.

As the night wore on and the revelry continued past midnight, the old man—now thoroughly drunk—stumbled towards the eastern part of the village. He vanished into the thick woods, making his way to a dark cave where he slept off the effects of the alcohol.

The following morning, Linani awoke and opened the container to check on Selah. The poor girl had spent a sleepless night, curled up in the cramped space, shivering from the cold. Her eyes were red with exhaustion, her spirit nearly broken.

Linani threw a few ripe bananas into the container, slamming the lid shut once more. It then transformed back into the guise of an old man, slinging a litungu—a traditional musical instrument—over its shoulder and carrying the container on its back. The creature set off towards neighboring villages, eager for more entertainment and free beer.

For three long weeks, this horrific cycle continued. Selah was trapped in the container, her songs forced out of her by the ogre's cruel demands. Each day brought new torment as *Linani* used her voice to entertain villagers, all while she remained a prisoner in the tiny, suffocating space. Her hope dwindled with each passing day, but deep within her, a spark of resilience refused to be extinguished.

v). The Great Search

For three long weeks, the village of Wesakulila was filled with sorrow and anxiety over the mysterious disappearance of Selah. Elder Mukari, his wife Khalayi, and their neighbors left no stone unturned in their search for her. They scoured every corner of the village, combing through forests and fields, asking every passerby if they had seen the beautiful girl. Despite their efforts, all they found was Selah's water pot abandoned near the spring. No one had any news about her whereabouts, and a dark cloud of despair settled over the village.

Elder Mukari, a man of great influence, even sought the intervention of community chief. Warriors were dispatched to scour distant lands, but they returned empty-handed, without any trace of the missing girl or clues to her fate. In his desperation, Elder Mukari made a bold declaration: "Whoever finds my daughter and brings her back home shall have her hand in marriage." But even this promise did not yield results, and the village seemed to lose hope.

One fateful evening, the search for Selah took a surprising turn. Elder Kundu's wife, Namaondo, was running her local brew joint as usual when a peculiar customer arrived. The customer was an old man, hunched over and armed with a litungu slung across his back and a container hanging by his side. Namaondo, a sharp-eyed and observant woman, immediately sensed something unusual about this man.

"Namaondo!" the old man called out as he approached, "I need a word with you before I settle in for a drink."

Namaondo nodded, leading him aside for a brief conversation. The old man spoke in a low, gravelly voice and insisted on sitting in the joint's front seat, right in the heart of the action. As soon as he was seated, he knocked on the container with his knuckles three times and began playing his litungu, the rhythm of the strings melding seamlessly with the beautiful voice that emerged from the container.

Before coming to Namaondo's joint, the old man had made a special arrangement with his crew. He had told them to make a fire and prepare a huge pot of boiling water because he would return home with a feast of fresh meat. It was clear he had something sinister in mind, but for now, he was focused on the music and the brew.

As the melodic sounds of the litungu filled the air, Namaondo's joint began to fill up with villagers, all eager to enjoy a night of dance and Bukusu's famous local brew, busaa. The old man's litungu playing was enchanting, and as the rhythm picked up, more people joined in, dancing and cheering. In the midst of this lively atmosphere, Selah's voice resonated clearly from within the container:

Nalekha esimbi yange Mumwalo
Nalekha esimbi yange Mumwalo
Bachi Njakhucheka kwenye machi kwikhale
Bachi Njakhucheka kwenye machi kwikhale

The crowd was captivated by the song's haunting beauty, but none were more attentive than Namaondo. She listened carefully, her eyes narrowing with suspicion as she recognized the lyrics. A sudden realization struck her like lightning. She remembered the stories surrounding Selah's disappearance and instantly felt a chill down her spine. Was this the missing girl singing from within that container?

Determined to find out the truth, Namaondo quietly called one of her sons over and whispered instructions to him. "Go, fetch Khalayi and Elder Mukari. Tell them to come quickly. I believe Selah is in that container."

Moments later, Khalayi, Elder Mukari, and a few other family members arrived at the joint. They listened intently as the music continued, and soon they, too, recognized Selah's voice. Their hearts raced with both relief and anger as they quickly devised a plan to rescue their daughter.

Khalayi decided to act fast. She asked her close friend, Namikoye, to take some of Namaondo's beer back to her home and host a small gathering. Meanwhile, Elder Mukari spoke to a few of the men present in the joint, inviting them to his home for a continuation of the night's drinking festivities. Namaondo, following the plan, made a loud announcement to the customers in her joint, "Friends, my gallons are empty! But not to worry, there is a fresh supply of the finest local brew in a neighbor's house!"

The crowd, now quite tipsy and eager for more drink, quickly agreed to move to the new location. Sensing that something was amiss, the old man tried to pick up his container and litungu to leave with the crowd. However, Namaondo, ever clever and convincing, approached him with a smile. "Why carry all that weight around, old man? You can leave your things here. We're all just going next door, and they'll be safe with me."

The old man hesitated for a moment, his eyes darting suspiciously. But the crowd was getting restless, and he didn't want to lose his chance to keep them entertained and drinking, so he reluctantly agreed. Namaondo watched closely as he stepped out, making sure to keep the container behind.

As soon as the old man was out of sight, Namaondo and Khalayi moved quickly. They opened the container with bated breath, and there, cramped and trembling, was Selah—pale, exhausted, and visibly shaken but very much alive. Khalayi burst into tears, hugging her daughter tightly as Elder Mukari stood in shock, overwhelmed by the sight of his lost child.

Selah's voice, weak but filled with relief, whispered, "Mama... Papa... you found me."

"Yes, my daughter," Khalayi sobbed, "and we'll never let you go again."

Elder Mukari, now fueled with both joy and fury, vowed to make the *Linani* pay for his evil deeds. "This creature will not torment our family or our village ever again," he declared, his voice filled with determination.

With Selah finally safe in their arms, the villagers began to plot how they would deal with the wicked *Linani* once and for all.

vi). Uncovering Selah's Whereabouts

As soon as Namaondo and Khalayi had seen the strange old man leave for Elder Mukari's home, they wasted no time. With swift hands, they opened the container and lifted their frail daughter, Selah, out of the cramped space. She was weak, her body trembling from exhaustion and fear, but her eyes lit up with relief as she saw her mother and Namaondo. Gently, they carried her to a nearby stream, where they bathed her, washing away the grime and misery of the last three weeks. Once she was clean, they hid her safely in a secret chamber inside Namaondo's home.

Knowing they needed to buy time and deceive the *Linani*, they quickly devised a clever plan. They found a heavy stone roughly the same weight as Selah and tied several layers of clothes around it to mimic the feel of a person. To further fool the ogre, they placed the stone back inside the container. Alongside it, they placed an esienene—a large, clever singing insect known for its ability to mimic sounds. Namaondo and Khalayi patiently taught the esienene the songs that Selah used to sing. The insect, with its innate ability, mastered them quickly.

Not long after, the old man returned. His eyes, shifty and suspicious, darted around as he approached Namaondo's house. He knocked on the container three times to ensure his captive was still inside. With a flutter of its wings, the esienene began singing:

Nalekha esimbi yange Mumwalo
Nalekha esimbi yange Mumwalo
Bachi Njakhucheka kwenye machi kwikhale
Bachi Njakhucheka kwenye machi kwikhale

The old man's face relaxed, and he chuckled, pleased with the sound of the familiar tune. He thanked Namaondo for her hospitality and hoisted the container onto his back, unaware that his captive had already escaped. With a crooked grin, he trudged away, heading back to his dark cave, where his fellow ogres eagerly awaited the promised feast.

Back in Wesakulila, Elder Mukari and the community chief were not resting either. The moment they received news of the old man's departure, they had already rallied a team of seasoned warriors. Armed with spears, shields, and flaming torches, they prepared to follow the old man into the depths of the forest. Their mission was clear: wipe out the ogres and ensure they never terrorize their village again.

Meanwhile, the old man, now transformed back into his true form as a giant ogre, finally reached his cave. His fellow ogres, anticipating a meal of fresh human flesh, surrounded him with greedy eyes and growling bellies. With a triumphant roar, the *Linani* opened the container to drop what he thought was Selah into a boiling pot of water. But instead of a helpless girl, a heavy stone plunged into the bubbling water, splashing scalding liquid everywhere. The esienene flew out, hovering above them with a mocking grin.

The cave erupted in chaos. The ogres snarled and growled in fury, turning on the old man who had promised them a feast. "You lied to us!" they bellowed, their voices echoing off the cave walls. "There is no girl here, just a stone and a foolish insect!"

Just as the argument among the ogres reached a fever pitch, the warriors from Wesakulila, who had stealthily tracked the old man to the cave, charged in. With a war cry that shook the earth, they attacked. The cave turned into a brutal battlefield as spears flew and blades slashed through the air. One by one, the warriors struck down the ogres, showing no mercy. The ogres, taken by surprise and weakened by their internal conflict, were no match for the skilled warriors. Soon, the cave floor was littered with the bodies of the fallen *Linani*.

To ensure that no trace of evil remained, the warriors set the cave ablaze. The flames roared to life, consuming everything inside, including the vile memories of the terror that the ogres had spread. As a final act of victory, they took the head of the deceitful old man to bring back to the village as proof of their triumph.

Back in Wesakulila, a wave of relief and celebration swept over the village. Elder Mukari and his family gathered at Namaondo's home, overwhelmed with gratitude. "Thank you, Namaondo," Elder Mukari said, his voice thick with emotion. "You helped save our beautiful daughter from that vile creature."

Selah embraced her parents as word of her rescue and the defeat of the ogres spread quickly through the village. Soon, the community began to turn against Nandako and her friends, who had not only refused to help Selah retrieve her missing necklace but had spread false and damaging rumors about her.

The community chief, a man known for his fairness, called Nandako and her friends to account for their actions. "You not only abandoned your friend in her time of need but also tried to tarnish her good name. Such behavior will not be tolerated in our village," he declared sternly.

As punishment, Nandako and her friends were ordered to work on Elder Mukari's family land for two full planting seasons, tilling the soil and tending to the crops. This act of penance served as a stark reminder to the entire community about the consequences of jealousy and malice. From that day forward, the villagers of Wesakulila learned to nurture love and respect, ensuring that no ill will or envy took root among them.

With the dark days behind them, the village once again became a place of harmony and joy, and Selah, the girl who had been tested by fire, shone even brighter with her spirit and resilience.

Natela Learns Her Lesson the Hard Way

i). Contradicting Worldviews

In a small, peaceful village surrounded by rolling hills and lush greenery, there lived two girls named Esinas and Natela. They were close friends who often spent their days playing together and helping each other with their daily chores. Though they shared many things in common, their hearts were very different. Esinas was known throughout the village for her empathy and kindness. She always considered the well-being of others above her own and was grateful for the simple things life offered. She believed that happiness was not found in material wealth but in the love and care shared with others.

Natela, on the other hand, had a very different outlook on life. She was filled with envy, always desiring the best of everything for herself, no matter the cost or consequence. She was never satisfied with what she had and often looked at Esinas with jealousy, wishing she could possess the same calm and contentment that seemed to radiate from her friend.

One sunny afternoon, Esinas was feeding her pet, Wanami, a gentle and clever hare, in the bushes near her family's cassava plantation. She loved this spot; it was quiet and peaceful, filled with the soft rustle of leaves and the chirping of birds. While she was distracted, feeding Wanami fresh greens, she suddenly felt a strange sensation under her feet. Before she knew it, she slipped and tumbled into a hidden, magical world—a place where the air was filled with an otherworldly glow and everything seemed to shimmer with a soft, golden light.

As Esinas got up and dusted herself off, she realized she was surrounded by a group of hares, all chattering in a language she could strangely understand. Wanami, her pet hare, stood among them, looking more regal and wise than ever before. With a calm and welcoming tone, Wanami spoke to her, "Welcome, Esinas, to the Wonder World. Please, follow me."

Esinas trusted Wanami despite intense fear and feeling of uncertainty about the pet. She followed this slowly, her eyes wide with awe as she walked through this enchanting new place. The path led them to a bright, glowing spot in the distance, and as they approached, the light became more intense but somehow soothing to her eyes.

From within this glowing light, a radiant hare emerged, its fur shimmering like sunlight on water, and its voice as soft as a lullaby. The glowing hare looked at Esinas with gentle eyes and presented her with two boxes. One box was wrapped in materials that glittered and shone with bright colors, catching the eye like a precious jewel. The other box, in stark contrast, was wrapped in plain, unassuming cloth—simple and ordinary.

The radiant hare spoke softly, "Esinas, you may choose one of these boxes. Choose wisely."

Esinas looked at both boxes carefully. While the brightly wrapped box dazzled and tempted her, she felt drawn to the plain one. She knew that beauty was not always on the surface and that what mattered was often hidden beneath. She reached out and chose the box wrapped in simple, ordinary cloth.

The glowing hare nodded approvingly. "Why did you choose this one, Esinas, instead of the bright and beautiful one?" it asked.

Esinas smiled gently and replied, "I believe that what is inside matters more than what is outside. I value what is hidden in the heart, not what merely shines on the surface."

The glowing hare's eyes sparkled with pride. "You have made a wise choice, Esinas. This box will bring you something special, but remember—open it only when you are home and tell no one about this gift or what you have experienced here today."

Esinas nodded, accepting the glowing hare's words. With Wanami by her side, she turned back; ready to return home with her mysterious gift and the wisdom she had gained from this extraordinary encounter.

ii). Esinas in the Wonderland

After thanking the glowing hare for the incredible adventure, Esinas followed Wanami, her loyal pet hare, back through the path they had come from. The bright light gradually faded away as they moved, and soon, Esinas found herself standing in her father's cassava plantation, holding the mysterious box from the wonderland. For a moment, she wondered if it had all been a dream. The familiar surroundings, the sight of Wanami munching on sweet potato vines, and the soft rustling of the cassava leaves felt so ordinary, so real.

But the weight of the box in her hands told a different story. It was real, and whatever lay inside it carried a promise of something beyond her imagination. Her heart pounded with a mix of excitement and curiosity. Without wasting another moment, she rushed back to her house, her mind racing with thoughts of what could be inside.

Once home, Esinas quietly locked herself in her bedroom, away from the prying eyes of her neighbors and friends. She took a deep breath and opened the box, her hands trembling slightly. As the lid lifted, a soft, golden light began to glow from within. To her amazement, the box started filling with all kinds of beautiful golden jewelry, clothes of the finest fabrics, and shoes that sparkled like the stars.

Esinas was overwhelmed by the sight. She felt like she was dreaming again. Instead of hastily grabbing the treasures, she decided to take only one item at a time. She chose a delicate golden bracelet and slipped it onto her wrist, feeling its cool weight against her skin. Carefully, she closed the box, as if fearing the magic might disappear if she were too greedy. She then hid the box under her bed, ensuring its safety and secrecy.

Over the next few days, Esinas' parents, Elder Watta and his wife, began to notice the new and beautiful things their daughter wore. She had fine clothes, sparkling jewelry, and new shoes that seemed too luxurious for their simple village life. They were intrigued but chose not to pry. They trusted Esinas's judgment and knew she was not one to engage in dishonest or deceitful acts.

Seeing how much her parents respected her privacy and trusted her, Esinas decided to share a part of her fortune with them. She reached into the magic box and took out a golden stone—a shimmering piece that looked as if it was made from the very essence of the sun. She presented it to her father, Elder Watta, with a simple explanation: "I found this in a special place. I believe it can help us."

Elder Watta, though curious about how his daughter came upon such a treasure, respected her silence and trusted her words. He decided to take the golden stone to Mzee Khalifa, the most renowned mineral dealer in the neighboring village. Mzee Khalifa, upon seeing the stone, was left in awe. It was a precious and rare gem, something he had never encountered before. After much negotiation, Elder Watta exchanged the stone for a significant amount of money.

When he returned home, Elder Watta used this newfound wealth wisely. He transformed their modest family house into a palatial residence. The compound once filled with the sounds of simple village life, now stood as a magnificent estate that left the entire village in awe. Beautiful gardens bloomed in the front yard, the walls were painted with vibrant colors, and the roof was adorned with a shining, metallic finish that gleamed in the sunlight. The villagers couldn't believe their eyes; whispers spread about the sudden fortune that had blessed Elder Watta's household.

Esinas watched all this unfold with a grateful heart. She never sought the wealth, yet it had found her due to her humble spirit and kind heart. She knew that the box was a gift, one that brought her family great fortune, but she remained cautious, aware of the responsibility that came with such power.

iii). The Price of Greed

The sudden transformation in Esinas' life did not go unnoticed by her best friend, Natela. Unlike Esinas, who was content with life's simple pleasures, Natela's heart burned with envy. She couldn't understand how Esinas had suddenly come into such fortune. Her jealousy grew each day, and she became determined to uncover Esinas' secret, hoping to gain the same fortune or even more.

Natela began to monitor Esinas' every move. She watched her from a distance, noting all the places she went and the things she did. One day, Natela saw Esinas heading towards her family's cassava plantation, where her pet hare, Wanami, was kept. She watched Esinas spend the entire day there, playing with Wanami and occasionally feeding it with sweet potato vines.

After Esinas left, Natela saw her chance. She sneaked into the field with her heart racing with anticipation. She had brought with her some special weeds she believed would entice Wanami. As soon as Wanami took the first bite of Natela's vines, a swirling light appeared, and they both transcended into the magical world. Natela couldn't believe her eyes. She had finally discovered the secret behind Esinas' sudden wealth!

Within moments, Natela found herself surrounded by hares, just like Esinas had been. Wanami, the hare, hopped beside her, guiding her towards the bright section ahead. Natela was ecstatic. Her heart raced with excitement, knowing she would soon be rich like Esinas. As they approached the bright spot, the glowing, soft-speaking hare appeared, just as it had to Esinas. It presented Natela with two boxes, wrapped in different materials: one was brightly colored, and the other looked plain and simple.

Without hesitation, Natela reached for the brightly colored box, her eyes gleaming with greed. She was sure that the more beautiful box contained the most valuable treasures. She tried to open it right away, eager to see what was inside, but the glowing hare stopped her. "You may open it only when you get back," it said in a calm yet commanding voice. Despite this, Natela couldn't resist the urge. As she was being escorted out of the wonderland, she fiddled with the lid, trying to sneak a peek at the treasures inside.

By the time she reached the cassava field, Natela had already pried open the box. She eagerly looked inside, hoping to find gold, jewels, or something precious. To her utter shock, the box was empty. She stared at it in disbelief, thinking it was some kind of trick. Determined to prove otherwise, she rushed home, holding the box tightly against her chest.

Once inside her bedroom, Natela hurriedly shut the door behind her. She sat on her bed and opened the box once more, hoping that something valuable would appear now that she was home. However, instead of treasures, she found a small jar of strange-looking body cream sitting inside the box. Natela became confused but hopeful that the cream might be magical and could bring her fortune if she applied it to her body.

Without a second thought, she dipped her fingers into the cream and smeared it all over her body. At first, nothing happened. But within minutes, Natela felt a strange itching sensation all over her skin. She looked down and gasped in horror as strange boils began to form, covering her entire body. The boils were large, red, and filled with pus, making her look like a patient afflicted with a terrible disease, similar to monkeypox. She screamed in terror, her voice echoing through the house.

Panicking, Natela shouted at the magic box, demanding it restore her body to normal. But no matter how much she yelled or pleaded, the box remained unresponsive. It lay on the floor, silent and empty, mocking her. Her screams soon attracted the attention of her parents, who burst into her room to find their daughter covered in horrifying boils.

When they tried to get an explanation from Natela, she struggled to convince them of what had happened. The mysterious disappearance of the magic box and Wanami from Esinas' cassava field only added to their confusion. The more Natela tried to explain, the less sense she made. Word of Natela's strange condition spread throughout the village, and soon the entire community began to see her situation as a psychotic episode requiring special therapy. Her friends started avoiding her, horrified by her terrible facial appearance and the unfortunate fate that had befallen her.

Natela learned a harsh lesson that day—that envy and greed can lead to one's downfall. She had tried to take what did not belong to her, only to end up losing everything she valued: her beauty, her friends, and her reputation. Meanwhile, Esinas continued to live a humble and fulfilling life, surrounded by people who loved and respected her for who she was.

<u>End</u>

Origin of Bukusu Knife (Embalu)

i). Mango's Birth and its Significance to Bukusu Culture

The village of Namarome was abuzz with excitement as the two-week celebration began. Colorful decorations adorned every hut, and the aroma of roasting meat and freshly baked bread filled the air. Drummers played lively rhythms, and the rhythmic clapping and singing of the villagers created an atmosphere of pure joy.

Mango's arrival was a cause for great celebration. The villagers, along with the chief's many wives, gathered around the hearth where the baby was laid in a beautifully crafted cradle. Omukhurarwa, beaming with pride, offered sacrifices to the ancestors, thanking them for the precious gift of a son.

Among the guests were the elders of the clan, who came with traditional gifts and blessings for the newborn. They presented Mango with a ceremonial cloak made of the finest animal skins, symbolizing his future role as the heir to the chieftaincy.

As the days passed, the celebration continued with traditional dances, storytelling, and competitions. Mango's presence was a beacon of hope for the people, who saw in him the promise of a strong and wise leader who would one day carry on the legacy of his father.

Yet, amid the joy, there were whispers of concern among the elders. They knew that Mango's path to becoming chief would not be an easy one. The title of chief was not only about lineage but also about proving oneself worthy through trials and wisdom.

One evening, as the celebrations drew to a close, the chief gathered his family and close advisors for a private meeting. His face was solemn as he addressed them.

"The time has come for us to ensure that Mango is prepared for the responsibilities that await him," Omukhurarwa said. "We must guide him and teach him the ways of leadership and the traditions of our people."

His words were met with murmurs of agreement, and plans were set in motion for Mango's upbringing and education. However, Mango did not know the immense challenges and revelations ahead of him and their impact on his destiny and test the unity of his family and tribe.

ii). Preparation for Future Roles

As Mango grew, his training to become the future leader of his people became a central focus. The elders and wise men of the Bukusu clan took on the monumental task of shaping him into a leader who would honor their traditions and guide his people with wisdom and strength.

The first step in Mango's education was to immerse him in the rich Bantu African traditional culture. He learned about the core values of his people—respect for elders, the importance of family, and the sacredness of the land. The elders taught him the customs and rituals that held his community together, from the ceremonies that marked important life events to the stories that conveyed the history and morals of the clan.

Mango also learned about his role in the complex social structure of his society. He was introduced to the different levels of the community—from the wise elders and respected leaders to the hardworking farmers and skilled artisans. He was taught how to interact with each group, understanding their needs and concerns while exercising his authority with fairness and compassion.

Training to become a strong warrior was another crucial part of Mango's preparation. The village's finest warriors took him under their wing, teaching him the art of combat. He learned how to wield traditional weapons like spears and bows with precision and skill. The blacksmiths showed him the secrets of transforming raw iron into finely crafted weapons, a skill that was vital for defending the community and leading them through times of conflict.

Mango's education also extended to agriculture. The elders stressed the importance of ensuring food security for his people. He learned about planting and harvesting crops, the significance of seasonal patterns, and the techniques to enrich the soil. He saw firsthand how agriculture was not just about growing food but about sustaining the life and prosperity of the entire community.

In addition to practical skills, Mango was taught to be a visionary leader. He learned the importance of diplomacy and forging alliances with neighboring communities. The art of negotiation and maintaining peace was as vital as the strength of a warrior. Mango practiced engaging with leaders from other clans, understanding their customs, and building relationships that would benefit his people.

As the years passed, Mango grew into a capable young man, ready to take on the responsibilities that lay ahead. His training had equipped him with the knowledge, skills, and wisdom to lead his people with honor and integrity. Yet, the true test of his leadership was yet to come, and Mango would soon face challenges that would reveal the depth of his character and the strength of his spirit.

iii). A Horrifying Invasion

The tranquility of the Whispering Woods was shattered one fateful night. A chilling wind swept through the village of Bungoma, carrying with it a sense of foreboding. The villagers, nestled in their huts after a long day of work and celebration, were abruptly awakened by the sound of terrified cries.

As dawn broke, the scene that greeted them was one of utter devastation. The once bustling livestock pens were now eerily empty. Sheep, goats, cattle—all had vanished without a trace. The villagers rushed to the scene, their faces pale with shock and fear.

Word quickly spread through the village: the ancient serpent, *Ekhilakhima,* had returned. For generations, *Ekhilakhima* had been nothing more than a terrifying tale told to children to keep them in line—a creature of legend, a monster whispered about in hushed tones around the campfire. The elders spoke of its malevolence, a beast so fearsome that even the bravest warriors dared not speak its name aloud.

Omukhurarwa, the revered chief, was deeply troubled. The disappearance of the livestock was a dire blow to the village's food security and economy. Without their animals, the people faced a future of hunger and hardship. The once-told tales of *Ekhilakhima* were now a grim reality, and the community was gripped by fear.

The night fell heavily on Bungoma as the village gathered in the central clearing. The once joyful place of celebration was now filled with anxiety and fear. The looming threat of *Ekhilakhima* had cast a dark shadow over the community. Chief Omukhurarwa, though usually a pillar of strength, found himself at a loss.

He addressed the villagers, his voice steady but tinged with concern. "We face a grave danger. Should we consider migrating to safer lands, or do we confront this serpent and protect our home?"

The villagers remained silent. Their faces, etched with fear, looked down at the ground. The tales of *Ekhilakhima* had instilled such terror that no one was willing to speak up, let alone challenge the serpent. Each person was paralyzed by the thought of facing the mythical beast they had only heard about in stories.

As the chief's question hung in the air, the ground shook with a low rumble. The serpent had returned, and this time, it was more ferocious than before. *Ekhilakhima* slithered through the village, its scales reflecting the moonlight like molten silver. The serpent's hiss echoed through the night, and screams pierced the darkness as the creature's wrath descended upon the community. The serpent's attack was devastating, leaving behind a scene of chaos and despair.

iv). Panic in the Bukusu Land

In the aftermath, the chief's heart ached with the loss of his people. The once-thriving village was now a place of mourning. Desperation gripped Omukhurarwa as he faced the harsh reality. He made the difficult decision to move the remaining population away from their beloved home. The journey to the neighboring Cherenganyi Hills was arduous, and the community clung to the hope that they would find safety and escape the serpent's reach.

However, fate had other plans. *Ekhilakhima* followed them, undeterred by the relocation. The serpent struck again, and this time, it was even more ruthless. The attack left only a handful of survivors, further diminishing the once-thriving village.

During this turmoil, Mango was away on a critical mission of his own. Seeking a solution to the serpent's menace, he had ventured to the other side of the Cherenganyi Hills to seek out his father's old friend and master iron-smelter, Cheptais. Cheptais was a renowned blacksmith with unparalleled skills in crafting weapons from iron.

Mango had learned of Cheptais' expertise and hoped that the knowledge of forging powerful weapons might provide the means to defend his people. Under Cheptais' meticulous guidance, Mango was taught the ancient art of iron-smelting. He learned how to transform raw iron into finely crafted spears, arrows, and other weapons that could stand against formidable adversaries.

The lessons were demanding and required great skill and patience. Mango worked tirelessly, driven by the urgency of the situation and the need to protect his community. His training not only strengthened his resolve but also equipped him with the tools needed to confront *Ekhilakhima*.

Back in the village, the remnants of the community clung to their hope, waiting for Mango's return. The serpent's relentless attacks had left them weary and frightened, but Mango's preparations were their beacon of hope. As Mango completed his training and forged the weapons, he knew that the time to face *Ekhilakhima* was drawing near.

With his new skills and a heart full of determination, Mango prepared to return to his people. He was ready to lead them in a fight for survival and reclaim their home from the ancient terror that had haunted their ancestors' tales. The fate of the village rested on his shoulders, and he was determined to rise to the challenge.

v). Preparation for the Hunt

Mango's return to the village was met with a mix of hope and despair. The sight that greeted him was heart-wrenching. The once vibrant community was now a shadow of its former self. The survivors, weary and grieving, looked to Mango with tear-filled eyes as he stepped into the village.

As Mango walked through the village, the people rushed to him, their voices a chorus of anguish. They wept openly, sharing their pain and fear. Mango's heart ached to see the devastation that had befallen his people. The serpent's relentless attacks had taken a severe toll, and the spirit of the community was at its lowest.

Determined to make a difference, Mango went straight to his father, Omukhurarwa. The chief sat among the ruins of what was once the heart of their village, his face lined with worry and sadness. Mango approached him, his own grief masked by a steely resolve.

"Father," Mango said his voice steady despite the turmoil inside him. "I have returned with the knowledge and weapons needed to fight Ekhilakhima. I ask for your blessing to confront the serpent and save our people."

Omukhurarwa's eyes were filled with uncertainty. The memory of their previous encounters with the serpent was fresh, and the thought of sending his son into such danger was painful. The chief had been struggling with the weight of the decisions he had to make and the loss that had already occurred.

At first, Omukhurarwa hesitated. The idea of Mango facing the serpent seemed daunting, even with the new weapons. The fear of losing more loved ones weighed heavily on his heart. But as he looked at Mango—now a young man forged by training and determination—he saw the resolve and courage that had grown within him.

After a moment of contemplation, Omukhurarwa made his decision. "Mango," he said, his voice resolute but filled with pride; "I have watched you grow into a leader and a warrior. If you believe that you can defeat *Ekhilakhima* and save our people, then I will give you my blessing. Prepare yourself and our people for the task ahead."

He then called for a gathering of the community. The villagers assembled around the central clearing, their faces marked by fatigue but also by a glimmer of hope. Omukhurarwa addressed them, his voice echoing with authority.

"Our people have suffered greatly," he began, "and the threat of *Ekhilakhima* has cast a long shadow over our lives. My son, Mango, has returned with the knowledge and weapons we need to confront this serpent. He has our blessing and our support."

The villagers listened in silence, their expressions a mix of hope and apprehension. Omukhurarwa continued, "We must come together now to fortify Mango and prepare for the battle ahead. Our unity and strength are our greatest assets in this fight."

The community rallied to support Mango, working tirelessly to strengthen their defenses. They reinforced the barriers around the village and set up strategic positions for the upcoming confrontation. The blacksmiths, under Mango's guidance, made final adjustments to the weapons, ensuring they were ready for the fight.

Mango, equipped with the new iron weapons and surrounded by the support of his people, felt a renewed sense of purpose. He was determined to face *Ekhilakhima* and reclaim their village from the terror that had plagued them.

As the preparations continued, Mango's focus was unwavering. The time to confront the serpent was drawing near, and he knew that the battle would not only test his skills but also the unity and resilience of his people. With his father's blessing and the community's support, Mango prepared for the fight that would determine the fate of his village.

vi). The Great Hunt

With the village fortified and the community's support behind him, Mango led a group of fifty brave warriors towards the *Cherenganyi* Forest. The air was thick with tension as they marched, each step echoing with the anticipation of the impending confrontation with *Ekhilakhima*.

The forest loomed before them, a vast and shadowy expanse that seemed to stretch endlessly. The once familiar trees and undergrowth now appeared menacing and foreboding, their twisted branches reaching out like gnarled fingers. The warriors moved cautiously, their senses on high alert for any sign of the serpent.

As they journeyed deeper into the jungle, Mango and his men noticed an eerie silence that settled over the forest. The usual sounds of wildlife—the chirping of birds, the rustling of leaves the distant calls of animals—was conspicuously absent. The forest, usually teeming with life, was now a desolate place.

The warriors exchanged uneasy glances as they pressed on. The lack of animal sounds and the unnatural quiet only added to their growing unease. Mango's sharp eyes scanned the surroundings, but there was no sign of the serpent or any of the creatures that once inhabited this land. It was as if the entire forest had been drained of life.

The deeper they ventured, the more apparent it became that something terrible had happened. The ground was littered with the remains of smaller creatures—bones and fragments scattered as grim evidence of the serpent's feast. The warriors' hearts sank with each step as they realized the full extent of the serpent's wrath. The once-thriving jungle had become a graveyard, a testament to *Ekhilakhima's* devastating presence.

Mango paused to gather his thoughts and confer with his leading warriors. They huddled together, their faces grim as they contemplated their next move.

The silence was oppressive, and the weight of the task ahead felt even heavier. The serpent was a powerful and malevolent force, and the desolation around them spoke of its destructive power.

"We must proceed with caution," Mango instructed. "The serpent may be close, and we cannot afford to be caught off guard. Stay alert and keep your weapons ready."

The warriors nodded, their expressions reflecting both determination and fear. They continued their trek through the forest, their every step filled with a heightened sense of urgency. Mango led them with unwavering resolve, guided by the knowledge that their village and their people depended on their success.

As they moved further into the forest, Mango's thoughts were focused on the task at hand. He knew that finding *Ekhilakhima* would not be easy, but the survival of his people and the future of his village depended on their success. The serpent's reign of terror had to end, and Mango was prepared to confront it, no matter the cost.

The journey through the silent, lifeless forest felt endless. The warriors pressed on, driven by the hope of finding the serpent's lair and ending its reign of terror once and for all. The forest's eerie quiet seemed to mock their efforts, but Mango remained determined. The fate of his people rested on their shoulders, and he was resolute in his mission to restore peace and safety to his village.

vii). Mango's Relentless Determination

As Mango and his warriors ventured deeper into the heart of the *Cherenganyi* Forest, an unsettling silence continued to envelop them. The absence of wildlife had become more than just eerie; it was a chilling sign of the serpent's dominance. The dense canopy above offered little respite from the oppressive atmosphere below.

Suddenly, Mango's keen senses were alerted by an unfamiliar, pungent odor. It was strong and acrid, unlike anything he had encountered before. The smell seemed to pervade the very air they breathed, a rank stench that clung to their clothes and made their stomachs churn. Mango's mind raced back to the ancient stories his father had told him about *Ekhilakhima*.

The tales had spoken of a "strong odor" as a precursor to the serpent's presence—a sign that *Ekhilakhima* was near. The words echoed in Mango's memory, as if his father's voice was guiding him through the forest. The realization hit him with a cold clarity: they were close to the serpent's lair.

"Stay alert!" Mango called out to his warriors. "We are getting close. Keep your senses sharp and prepare yourselves."

But the dense undergrowth and the overpowering smell made the terrain treacherous. The warriors, despite their courage, struggled to navigate through the thick foliage. Their footing became unstable as the ground seemed to shift beneath them. Mango's heart pounded with urgency as he led the way, but the forest had other plans.

Without warning, several of Mango's men stumbled and fell into a concealed cave entrance. The ground gave way beneath them, and they plummeted into the darkness below. The cave was a horrifying sight—a pit filled with the remains of countless creatures. Dry, skeletal bones were scattered around, evidence of the serpent's horrific feasts. Some warriors fell directly onto these macabre remains, while others hit their heads on the jagged rocks, their deaths instant and brutal.

The cries and thuds of the fallen warriors echoed through the cave, a grim testament to the danger that lurked below. Mango's heart sank as he realized the extent of their peril. The cave was a death trap, a pitfall designed by the serpent to ensnare and devour its victims.

Desperate to avoid further casualties, Mango signaled the remaining warriors to halt. They formed a tight circle around the cave entrance, their faces etched with shock and grief. Mango felt a deep sense of responsibility for the lives lost and the danger that still loomed.

"We must find another way," Mango urged his remaining men. "We cannot afford to lose more of our own. We need to be cautious and use our wits."

The warriors, though shaken, nodded in agreement. They carefully retraced their steps, avoiding the perilous area around the cave. The overpowering smell continued to guide them, leading them further into the forest's depths.

Mango's mind was consumed with both the fear for his people and the resolve to see their mission through. The discovery of the cave and the loss of his men only reinforced his determination to confront *Ekhilakhima*. He knew that the serpent's lair was close, and the time to face the beast was drawing near.

The journey through the dark and foreboding forest tested their endurance and courage. Despite the fear and loss, Mango pressed on with unwavering resolve, driven by the memory of those who had fallen and the promise of reclaiming their village from the serpent's terror.

viii). An Encounter with Ekhilakhima

The strange, acrid odor grew stronger as Mango and his warriors made their way through the forest. It filled Mango's nostrils, a pungent reminder that they were nearing their formidable foe. His senses were heightened, every rustle and sound amplified in the tense silence that had settled over the forest.

As Mango prepared himself for the inevitable confrontation, the atmosphere was shattered by the sounds of breaking trees and the deep, resonant hissing of *Ekhilakhima*. The noise reverberated through the forest, a sinister prelude to the serpent's presence. Mango's heart raced as he steeled himself for the battle ahead.

Suddenly, Mango's eyes widened in disbelief. The forest clearing opened before him, and there, amidst the fallen trees and underbrush, laid the creature of legend. *Ekhilakhima*, the ancient serpent of the fairytales, was revealed in its full, terrifying glory. It was an enormous snake, its body sinuous and massive like an anaconda, but with features that defied belief.

The serpent's scales were a grotesque patchwork of red and black, its skin glistening with a menacing sheen. From its head sprouted long, twisted horns reminiscent of an impala's, and a set of beards hung from its jaw, adding to its fearsome visage. The creature's eyes burned with a malevolent intelligence, glowing like embers in the dim light of the forest.

Mango's breath caught in his throat as he lay hidden beneath a thick tree stump, his heart pounding in his chest. He had taken this position to observe and understand the serpent's behavior before making his move. The sight before him was both awe-inspiring and horrifying. The sheer size of *Ekhilakhima* and its fearsome appearance were beyond anything he had imagined.

The serpent's vast mouth opened wide in a hissing snarl, its tongue flicking in and out as it scanned the surroundings. The sound of its hissing was deafening, a reminder of the deadly force that lay in wait. Mango could see the immense power in its coiled muscles, the strength that had decimated his village and claimed the lives of his warriors.

As Mango observed, he noted the serpent's movements and patterns. *Ekhilakhima* seemed to be patrolling its territory, a dark ruler of the forest that had driven all other life away. Mango realized that the serpent was not merely a mindless beast; it was a cunning and strategic predator, its senses attuned to every disturbance in its domain.

Mango's hands tightened around the weapons he had forged. The time for hesitation was over. The terror of facing *Ekhilakhima* was matched only by his determination to end the serpent's reign. He knew that this confrontation would require all his courage, skill, and the support of his warriors. They had come too far and lost too much to turn back now.

With a deep breath, Mango prepared to emerge from his hiding place. He knew that he had to confront the serpent, not just for the survival of his people but to restore the peace and safety of their home. The path ahead was fraught with danger, but Mango was resolute. The battle with *Ekhilakhima* was about to begin, and he was ready to face the monster that had haunted the legends of his people

ix). A Strategic Plan to Neutralize the Serpent

For the next five days, Mango remained hidden in the dense foliage, observing the serpent with the keenest attention. The task was both exhausting and perilous, but Mango was determined to gather as much information as possible about *Ekhilakhima*. He understood that to defeat this ancient terror, he needed to understand it completely.

Mango meticulously noted the serpent's behaviors. He observed its feeding habits, noting that Ekhilakhima had a voracious appetite. It consumed not only the remains of smaller creatures but also seemed to have a preference for certain types of prey. The serpent would often disappear into the forest for hours before reappearing, its massive form swollen with its latest meal.

Resting patterns were equally revealing. The serpent had several hidden lairs within the forest, each camouflaged and well-concealed. It would frequently move between these resting places, making it difficult to predict its exact location. Mango noted that the serpent's lairs were lined with soft tree bark and leaves, which seemed to serve as makeshift bedding.

One of the most surprising discoveries came when Mango observed the serpent treating its own wounds. Ekhilakhima's body was scarred and marked by previous battles, but the serpent had developed an unusual method of self-care. Mango watched in astonishment as the creature chewed on certain types of leaves, which appeared to have a soothing effect on its wounds. Additionally, the serpent would rub its injuries against the soft bark of trees, a behavior that seemed to alleviate its pain.

Mango was particularly struck by the serpent's blood. Unlike the red blood of most creatures, *Ekhilakhima's* blood was a sickly greenish hue. This unique characteristic only added to the serpent's otherworldly nature. The green blood was a further testament to the creature's formidable and unnatural qualities.

Another striking feature Mango discovered was the serpent's protruding upper canine teeth. These elongated fangs were not only fearsome but appeared to be a key weapon in the serpent's arsenal. They were capable of inflicting deep, venomous bites, further enhancing the creature's danger.

Mango's most startling revelation came when he heard *Ekhilakhima* uttering words of anguish during moments of pain. The serpent's hisses and growls were interspersed with what sounded like actual words—painful, guttural expressions that seemed almost sentient. The ability of the serpent to vocalize its suffering was a chilling reminder of its intelligence and complexity.

These discoveries painted a picture of *Ekhilakhima* as more than just a beast of legend. It was a cunning, adaptive creature with unique behaviors and abilities. Mango knew that understanding these aspects was crucial to devising a strategy to defeat it.

With his observations complete, Mango was ready to act. The knowledge he had gained about the serpent's feeding habits, self-care practices, and physical characteristics would be essential in formulating a plan. He had witnessed the serpent's vulnerabilities and was prepared to use this information to confront the beast.

As Mango prepared to execute his plan, he felt a mixture of anticipation and resolve. The battle against *Ekhilakhima* was no longer just a fight for survival—it was a test of his leadership, strategy, and the resilience of his people. With the knowledge he had gathered, Mango was determined to face the serpent and reclaim peace for his village.

x). The Final Blow

On the final day of his meticulous preparations, Mango was ready to execute his daring plan. The cave where *Ekhilakhima* spent its nights was a cavernous, foreboding place, hidden deep within the forest and protected by the serpent's eerie presence. Mango knew that to defeat the beast, he needed to outwit it with a trap of unprecedented ingenuity.

Mango set to work with a sense of urgency and precision. At the depth of the cave, he planted a series of strong, sharp spears, each pointed skyward and arranged in such a way that they would pierce through any object that fell onto them. The spears were strategically placed to ensure that even the slightest weight would trigger their deadly tips. This trap was designed to catch *Ekhilakhima* off guard and inflict a critical blow.

In addition to the spears, Mango prepared another element of his trap. He cut and secured a massive log of wood above the spot where the serpent often rested. The log was positioned precariously, poised to fall and crush anything that lay beneath it. With the cave prepared, Mango made his final adjustments and took a moment to prepare for the task ahead.

Next, Mango ventured deep into the forest to find and provoke *Ekhilakhima*. The dense undergrowth and oppressive silence seemed to close in around him as he moved, but Mango's focus was unwavering. He knew that luring the serpent to the cave was crucial for the success of his plan.

After an arduous search, Mango finally spotted the serpent, its massive form undulating through the forest with an air of menacing authority. Without hesitation, Mango began to provoke Ekhilakhima, using loud shouts and deliberate movements to draw the creature's attention. The serpent's eyes glowed with fierce determination as it fixated on Mango, its hunger piqued by the challenge.

As Mango sprinted back towards the cave, Ekhilakhima gave chase with surprising speed. The forest floor trembled with the force of the serpent's movement, and Mango's heart pounded as he raced towards the trap he had set.

Upon reaching the entrance of the cave, Mango turned to face the serpent. *Ekhilakhima,* driven by its predatory instincts, lashed out with its massive tail. The strike was powerful and sudden, and Mango was thrown off balance like a mere leaf in the wind. He crashed into the trunk of a towering oak tree, the impact sending a jarring pain through his body. His sword flew from his grasp, landing several feet away.

The collision with the oak tree was brutal. Mango felt a searing pain as a huge piece of the tree splintered and pierced through his ankle. Blood began to ooze from the wound, mixing with the dirt and leaves on the forest floor. The agony was intense, and Mango's head throbbed from the impact.

Despite the pain, Mango's mind remained focused. He had to endure and stay conscious to ensure that his trap would work. The serpent was now within range of the cave, and Mango needed to hold on just a little longer.

With his strength waning, Mango struggled to drag himself closer to the cave's entrance. He fought through the pain, driven by the knowledge that the success of his plan depended on his ability to lure *Ekhilakhima* into the trap. The serpent, now fully enraged, slithered towards the cave, its massive form filling the entrance as it moved.

Mango could only hope that his carefully crafted trap would be enough to defeat the serpent and save his people. As he lay in agony, he silently urged the spears and the log to do their work. The moment of reckoning was near, and Mango's fate, as well as that of his village, hinged on the outcome of this deadly confrontation.

xi). Triumph in Bukusu Land

Mango, having been trained in the ways of leadership and strategy, felt a deep sense of responsibility. He knew that his father's position as chief and his own future leadership depended on finding a solution to this crisis. With his father's blessing, Mango took it upon himself to lead the effort to confront the serpent.

Wounded and exhausted, Mango summoned the last reserves of his strength. He crawled painfully on his back, dragging himself away from the cave and into the dense woods. His mind raced as he pondered his next move. The serpent's lair was now behind him, but he needed to find a way to ensure Ekhilakhima's defeat was final.

Unbeknownst to Mango, the serpent had begun its search for the attacker who had dared to challenge it. With a predatory grace, *Ekhilakhima* slithered through the forest, its enormous body undulating with each movement. The serpent's eyes narrowed as it detected Mango's legs, partially hidden beneath the underbrush.

With a swift, powerful motion, *Ekhilakhima's* tail swept beneath the foliage, lifting Mango into the air. The young warrior was suddenly exposed and defenseless, his injuries rendering him weak and vulnerable. The serpent's laughter echoed through the forest, a deep, rumbling sound filled with sarcasm and mockery.

"Foolish boy!" Ekhilakhima thundered. "Did you think you could defeat me so easily? You are nothing but a naïve child seeking death."

Despite his pain, Mango's eyes remained sharp. As he lay exposed, he noticed something crucial— a soft spot on the serpent's underbelly. The memory of his father's stories surfaced in his mind, recounting that Ekhilakhima's heart was the only delicate part of its otherwise impenetrable body.

Suddenly, *Ekhilakhima*'s tail struck Mango with a heavy blow, sending him tumbling toward the cave's entrance. In a stroke of fortune, Mango landed in a small hole he had dug that very morning, designed as a last-resort refuge. The hole provided him temporary shelter and a strategic advantage.

With a pained but defiant smile, Mango raised his head and mockingly taunted the serpent. "Is that all you've got, serpent? You're just a big, ugly creature hiding in the shadows!"

Enraged by Mango's insolence, *Ekhilakhima* lunged forward, its massive body hurtling toward the cave entrance in a furious attempt to crush the defiant warrior. But the serpent's rage worked against it. As Ekhilakhima leaped over Mango's head, it fell directly onto the sharp spears that Mango had set up earlier.

The spears pierced through the serpent's body with deadly precision. The creature let out a final, earth-shaking roar as it writhed in agony, its massive form convulsing uncontrollably. Mango watched with a mix of relief and grim satisfaction as Ekhilakhima's struggle grew weaker and weaker. Finally, the serpent's massive body laid still, the life draining from it.

Breathing heavily, Mango climbed out of the hole and approached the fallen serpent. With a determined effort, he took a ceremonial axe from his belt and chopped off Ekhilakhima's huge head. He carefully removed the serpent's tongue, a symbol of his victory and proof of the beast's defeat. With his trophies in hand, Mango made his way back to the village.

As Mango approached the village, the sight of him alive and bearing the serpent's tongue on his shoulder, sparked an overwhelming wave of joy and relief. The community, who had endured so much suffering, welcomed him with jubilant cheers and heartfelt celebrations. The mood was one of sheer exultation as Mango was greeted as a hero.

For seven days and nights, the Bukusu community celebrated their new beginning. They feasted, drank, and rejoiced in the victory over the serpent. The celebration was a testament to Mango's bravery and the resilience of the people who had faced such dire threats and emerged victorious.

Mango's triumph was not only a personal victory but a new chapter for the village. The fear of *Ekhilakhima* was replaced with a renewed sense of hope and unity. As the festivities continued, Mango looked forward to the future with a sense of accomplishment and pride, knowing that his people were safe and that a new era had begun.

xii). Mango Receives the Cut

On the last day of the grand celebration, the great chief, Omukhurarwa, stood before the gathered community, his voice commanding attention as he summoned Mango to step forward. The crowd, a sea of faces filled with admiration and respect, fell silent. All eyes turned to Mango, the young warrior whose bravery had saved them from the terror of *Ekhilakhima*.

The chief addressed his people, his voice strong and filled with pride. "Mango, son of the Bukusu clan, you have proven your courage and strength in ways that will be spoken of for generations. Your manhunt for the serpent was not for personal glory, but for the good of our community. You have restored peace to our land, and for that, we honor you today."

The crowd erupted into cheers, but the chief raised his hand for silence once more. "However, the elders and community leaders have come together and decided that such a warrior's name must be preserved for generations to come. To mark this new beginning for our Bukusu people, we request that you take the cut—be circumcised publicly—as a symbol of your passage into manhood and leadership."

Mango, with humility and respect, bowed before his father and the elders. He understood the weight of their request, but he objected, not out of fear, but out of his belief that his deeds should speak for themselves. However, the elders, steadfast in their decision, set the date for the circumcision ceremony, believing it to be a rite that would forever tie Mango's legacy to the cultural roots of the Bukusu.

When the first day of *Lwokhunane* (the month of August) arrived, a palpable sense of anticipation filled the village. That night, Mango stayed outside his hut, surrounded by the entire community—young and old, female and male, wealthy and poor—who sang and chanted his name in praise of his courage and determination. Their voices echoed through the night, a melodic tribute to the hero among them. The rhythmic beats of drums and songs of celebration filled the air, marking the night as one of reverence and unity.

As dawn broke, the crowd began to move toward the nearby river. There, the elders asked Mango to remove his attire and stand naked, as was tradition. The cold morning air bit at his skin, but he stood tall and unyielding, his face calm and resolute. Three elders from his maternal home smeared his body with clay from the riverbank, a symbolic gesture to cleanse him and prepare him for the ritual that lay ahead. The entire community, a living tide of support, escorted Mango back to the village.

Upon their return, a second crowd was waiting, gathered around *Etiang'i*, the sacred spot for the circumcision ritual. The *omukhebi*, the first circumciser, stood ready, his tools prepared with precision and care. As Mango approached *Etiang'i*, a hush fell over the crowd. The gravity of the moment settled upon everyone. He walked with a steady stride, his head held high, and positioned himself at the designated spot.

In a matter of seconds, the *omukhebi* moved with expert speed. Mango's foreskin was cut away cleanly and swiftly, and for a heartbeat, there was silence. Then, an eruption of cheers, songs, and chants filled the air as the community celebrated Mango's transition into manhood. His bravery was being honored, not just in battle, but in the way he embraced the deep traditions of his people.

Mango's circumcision marked the dawn of a new era—the beginning of the Bukusu circumcision age sets. From that day forward, he was known as *Omunyange,* a leader, a warrior, and a protector of his people. The songs of his courage and the story of his great hunt would be passed down from generation to generation, reminding the Bukusu of the power of bravery, unity, and tradition.

As the celebrations continued, Mango stood among his people, his body bearing the mark of his rite of passage. He had not only saved his community but also woven himself into the very fabric of their identity and heritage.

<u>End</u>

Kasawa and Liondo, the Mysterious Pumpkin Fruit

i). Kasawa's Mysterious Workplace

Long ago, in the lush village of Eluhyia, there lived a strong and skilled blacksmith named Kasawa. Known throughout the land for his unparalleled craftsmanship, Kasawa was the pride of his community. His muscular frame and hardened hands spoke of years spent hammering metal, shaping it into the tools and weapons that sustained the lives of the Bukusu people and their neighbors.

The fertile soil and favorable climate of the region allowed the Bukusu people to thrive. They cultivated vast fields of millet, sorghum, and sweet potatoes, and kept cattle that grazed on the green hills. To cultivate their land and protect their families, they relied on Kasawa's creations—the traditional ploughs, the metallic chains linking the ploughs to the yokes, and the sharp arrowheads and spears that could pierce even the toughest hides.

Kasawa was a man of honor, surrounded by the warmth of his four wives and his nineteen children, a true testament to the Bukusu culture that cherished family above all else. His compound was always filled with laughter, the rhythmic pounding of his hammer, and the crackling of his forge. But there was a secret place where Kasawa would often disappear to, a place known only to him and his gods—a mystical realm called *Mumbo*, said to exist in the skies.

In *Mumbo*, Kasawa would work on his finest creations, forging tools and weapons that seemed to hold the power of the gods themselves. None in the village knew of this place, not even his closest friend, Kisika, who had been with him through many rites of passage. When asked, Kasawa would simply smile and say, "The gods showed me this place after I became a man. It is where I find the strength to make tools that last for generations."

ii). Danger at Kasawa's Doorstep

In one of Kasawa's previous trips to the mystical realm of Mumbo, he returned with a strange, ripe pumpkin fruit unlike any he had seen before. The fruit was round and plump, with a smooth skin that shimmered with hues of violet and gold under the sunlight. Intrigued by its appearance, Kasawa decided to plant its seeds in his garden, believing they might have special medicinal properties or bring some unknown benefits to his family and the community.

Upon his return, he handed the pumpkin to his youngest wife, Nanderema, with specific instructions. "Extract the seeds from this fruit," he told her, "and dry them carefully. We will plant them in our garden so that they can produce many more fruits. Who knows what benefits these strange pumpkins may bring?"

Nanderema did as she was told, carefully extracting the seeds and drying them under the sun. Once dried, Kasawa planted them in a special section of his garden, hoping they would yield many fruits and seeds for future use. However, this pumpkin plant grew in a manner unlike any other. It expanded rapidly, its thick vines sprawling over the ground, and twisted around anything in their path. Strangely, it formed only one fruit—an enormous, mysterious pumpkin that seemed to pulse with an unusual energy.

Kasawa sensed something extraordinary about the plant. He gathered his wives and children one afternoon and, with a stern expression, warned them. "Listen carefully," he said, his deep voice echoing with authority. "This pumpkin plant is not like the others. I suspect it may be enchanted or have special properties. Under no circumstances should anyone go near it, let alone touch it. Do you all understand?"

His wives and children nodded in agreement, their eyes wide with curiosity and a hint of fear. The pumpkin fruit, large and luminous, seemed to hold a secret within, and it's strange aura was felt by all.

Soon after, with the upcoming planting season, Kasawa began receiving many requests for new farm equipment from villagers and neighboring communities. His reputation as the best blacksmith in the region meant that he was in high demand, and the orders were piling up.

One evening, as the sun dipped below the horizon, Kasawa gathered his wives and children around the fire. "I must go on a long journey back to my workplace in Mumbo," he told them. "The demand for tools

iii). Disobedience and Death in Kasawa's Home

At the crowing of the first cock, the sky still dark and the village wrapped in the mist of dawn, Kasawa set out for his journey to Mumbo. He believed his family was safe, trusting that his wives would keep a watchful eye on his children and the strange pumpkin plant in his absence. He trekked for hours, reaching the base of the Cherenganyi Hills just as the sun began to peek over the horizon, casting long shadows on the grassy slopes.

Kasawa paused and whistled a unique tune known only to him. Almost immediately, a mysterious ladder descended from the sky, its rungs shimmering like they were woven from the threads of the sun and moon. This was the secret ladder that took him to his mystical workshop in the skies, the place where the gods had blessed him with the art of blacksmithing.

Kasawa climbed the ladder, leaving the world below, and disappeared into the clouds above, ready to craft the tools and weapons that were in high demand for the forthcoming planting season.

Back in Eluhyia, for the first seven days, everything was calm. Kasawa's family carried out their daily routines, and his wives diligently managed the farm and household chores. Nabututu, his first wife, ensured that all the children stayed away from the mysterious pumpkin plant, as Kasawa had commanded.

On the fourth day, however, Nabututu needed to go to the nearby market to buy *kumunyu* (African traditional salt) to prepare a meal. Confident that all was well, she left the homestead, leaving the children playing in the fields while the other wives had gone to the farm to prepare the land for the new season.

While playing near the edge of the garden, Kasawa's third-born daughter, Namikoye, couldn't resist her growing curiosity. She was a spirited girl with a sense of adventure, and her mind kept drifting to the mysterious pumpkin plant that her father had forbidden them from approaching. "Why is Papa so secretive about this pumpkin?" she wondered. "It's just a liondo, after all."

Driven by this curiosity, Namikoye crept into the garden, glancing around to make sure no one was watching. As she approached, she saw the *huge and smooth liondo* (pumpkin fruit) lying there, ripe and inviting. It seemed to glow under the sunlight, almost as if calling out to her. She marveled at its size and beauty and wondered why such a large, mature pumpkin was right there in their garden when her heart and that of her siblings longed for the taste of liondo.

The temptation was too strong to resist. "What harm could it do?" she thought. With a quick glance over her shoulder, Namikoye reached out and plucked the giant pumpkin from its vine, ignoring the sense of unease creeping up her spine.

Unnoticed by anyone, Namikoye slipped into the kitchen, hiding the pumpkin from view. She took a sharp knife and, with some effort, sliced the liondo into large chunks, dropping them into a pot to boil. The aroma that filled the air was rich and sweet, unlike any other pumpkin they had ever cooked.

When the liondo was ready, she called out to her siblings, her eyes gleaming with excitement. "Come! I've prepared a treat for us—our favorite liondo!" she announced. The children, whose mouths watered at the thought of the delicious pumpkin, quickly washed their hands and crowded around the bowl.

All of them eagerly grabbed chunks of the liondo, their small hands diving in with greed, savoring the taste they had craved for so long. All except for Kasawa's lastborn child, Wekulo, doubted the source of this meal. "Are you sure we should be eating this?" he asked nervously. "Papa told us not to go near that pumpkin."

But his siblings, their mouths full and eyes closed in delight ignored his words. "Stop being such a coward, Wekulo," chided Namikoye, laughing as she devoured more of the liondo. "It's just a pumpkin, and it tastes amazing!"

However, Wekulo's unease grew as he watched his brothers and sisters eat. Suddenly, without warning, Namikoye's laughter turned into a gasp. Her eyes widened in shock, and she clutched her throat, choking. Before anyone could react, she fell to the ground, lifeless.

Panic swept through the children. But before they could cry out, Netondo, the next in line, started coughing violently and collapsed beside Namikoye.

Then Nanjakho followed, and soon, one by one, each child who had eaten the liondo fell to the ground, their faces contorted in pain.

Only Wekulo stood there, tears streaming down his face, horrified at what he had just witnessed. The warning from his father echoed in his mind, but it was too late. His siblings lay still, lifeless, around the bowl of the cursed liondo.

The strange pumpkin fruit that Kasawa had warned them about was no ordinary fruit—it was a test, a gift from the gods that held both great promise and terrible danger. The tragedy that unfolded was a harsh reminder that some mysteries are not meant to be unraveled by the curious or the impatient.

iv). The Mysterious White Pigeon

At first, Wekulo thought his siblings were playing a cruel prank on him. He nudged Namikoye with his foot, waiting for her to spring up with laughter, but she remained still. He touched her neck and felt no pulse. A wave of terror surged through him. Desperately, he checked each of his siblings, one by one, only to discover that none of them had a heartbeat. The horrifying truth sank in: they were all dead.

Panic gripped Wekulo's heart as he realized he was completely alone. His cries for help echoed across the homestead, but there was no response. Everyone—his mothers, the neighbors, everyone—was at the farm, far away from the compound. His voice carried through the empty fields, swallowed by the vast silence around him.

Frantic thoughts raced through his mind. "What do I do? How do I bring them back?" He searched his memory for any remedies, anything he had learned or heard that might reverse this tragedy. But nothing came to him. He was just a child, alone and terrified.

Suddenly, as if guided by some unseen force, a *white pigeon* landed in the middle of the playfield. Its feathers glistened like freshly fallen snow, and its black eyes seemed to pierce through Wekulo's fear. This was *Liusi,* the legendary bird known in village fairy tales for delivering important messages to distant places. It was said that Liusi could cross great distances faster than any human and that it was often sent by the gods themselves.

Wekulo's eyes widened with a spark of hope. He remembered the tales his father had told them by the fire—stories of Liusi carrying messages of great urgency to faraway lands and bringing back answers to desperate prayers. He took a cautious step toward the bird, and to his surprise, Liusi did not fly away. It stood calmly, as if waiting for him.

With tears streaming down his face, Wekulo rushed into the house. He grabbed a handful of *bulo* (sorghum grains) and poured them onto *lutelu* (a small traditional tray). He carried the mat back to the pigeon, his hands trembling with desperation. As he laid the grains in front of Liusi, the pigeon pecked at them, eating slowly but deliberately.

As Liusi ate, Wekulo began to sing a song, his voice trembling but growing stronger with each verse, his words flowing with a rhythm born from his heartache and hope:

> *"Nche Nche Nche Mumbo!*
> *Nche Nche Nche Mumbo, Nche Nche!*
> *Ncha Khulola Kasawa Nche Nche!*
> *Liondo nilio karaka Nche Nche!*
> *Liamalile bana Nche Nche!*
> *Likhumi na munane, Nche Nche!"*

The song was a call to his father, a lament for his lost siblings, and a desperate plea for help. His voice carried over the fields, a haunting melody filled with sorrow. The pigeon seemed to understand the urgency in Wekulo's voice, and with every gulp of *bulo*, it bobbed its head to the rhythm of his song.

By the time Liusi had finished eating, the bird lifted its wings, stretched them wide, and took flight. It soared high above the homestead, heading towards *Mumbo,* the mystical place where Kasawa was busy crafting in his secret workshop. As it flew, Liusi repeated Wekulo's song, carrying the mournful tune across the sky.

Wekulo watched until the white pigeon was just a dot in the distance. His heart was heavy with worry, but he clung to a fragile thread of hope. "Please, Liusi, reach my father," he whispered. "Please bring him back to save us."

And so, he waited, alone among the lifeless bodies of his siblings, his eyes fixed on the sky, praying for a miracle.

v). Disseminating the Message

Nabututu, Kasawa's first wife, was on her way back from the market, her basket filled with *kumunyu* (African salt) and other supplies she had purchased for the family. She was walking briskly, eager to return home and begin preparing a meal, when she heard a faint, melodic sound coming from above.

She looked up and saw *Liusi,* the white pigeon, flying overhead, singing a sorrowful song that echoed through the skies:

Nche Nche Nche Mumbo!
Nche Nche Nche Mumbo, Nche Nche!
Ncha Khulola Kasawa Nche Nche!
Liondo nilio karaka Nche Nche!
Liamalile bana Nche Nche!
Likhumi na munane, Nche Nche!"

At first, Nabututu didn't understand the meaning of the song. The words were cryptic, but there was something familiar about them. She continued on her path, her heart beginning to beat faster with a sense of unease. As the song continued, the lyrics began to piece together in her mind, each word connecting to a fragment of memory—Kasawa's warning, the mysterious *liondo,* and their children. Suddenly, a chill ran down her spine as realization dawned upon her.

Without another thought, she broke into a sprint, her feet pounding the dusty path as she prayed desperately. "Please, let it not be true. Let nothing have happened to our children!" she whispered breathlessly, clutching the basket close to her chest.

Meanwhile, Kasawa's other wives—Namikoye and her two co-wives—were still at the farm, tending to the land, when they too heard *Liusi's* sorrowful song echoing across the fields. They paused and listened, confusion quickly turning into alarm as they recognized the familiar names in the lyrics. Their eyes widened in horror as they understood the implications of the song. Without a word, they dropped their tools and began running toward their home, their hearts pounding with dread.

As Nabututu reached the edge of the homestead, she saw a few villagers walking away from their compound. Their shoulders were raised, hands crossed towards their armpits, and they were shaking their heads in sadness. The sight froze her in her tracks. "No... Please, no..." she murmured, her mouth going dry with fear.

She forced her legs to move, pushing past the villagers, and finally, she reached the heart of her home. Her mouth fell open in horror. A large crowd had gathered, and in the middle of the compound lay the eighteen lifeless bodies of Kasawa's children, stretched out on the ground beside a large bowl filled with the remains of the *liondo*.

Nabututu felt her knees weaken. She stumbled forward, dropping her basket, and fell to her knees beside the bodies. Tears streamed down her face as she touched each child's cold cheek, her hands trembling. "No, no, no!" she wailed, her voice breaking with grief.

Moments later, Namikoye and the other co-wives arrived at the scene. They, too, were struck with disbelief and horror. "What has happened?" they cried out, rushing to join Nabututu beside the lifeless bodies. Their eyes widened, and they covered their mouths in shock. The truth was unbearable.

Desperate to save their children, the three wives began to pour cold water over the bodies, hoping against hope that the chill might somehow wake them, revive them from this nightmare. They whispered prayers, chanted incantations, and rubbed the cold limbs of their children, but their efforts were in vain. The children did not stir. The curse of the liondo had claimed them.

When the reality finally settled in that their children were gone, their grief quickly turned to anger. Namikoye and the other co-wives rounded on Nabututu, their faces contorted with fury. "This is your fault!" Namikoye shouted. "You were supposed to watch over the children! You failed us!"

"You let this happen! How could you be so careless?" cried another, her voice filled with anguish.

Nabututu, tears streaming down her cheeks, tried to defend herself. "I went to the market to get salt for us... I didn't think... I never imagined..." But her words were drowned out by the rising tide of anger and blame from her co-wives.

The crowd of villagers looked on in silence, their faces etched with sorrow and pity. The tragedy had not only shattered Kasawa's family but had also cast a shadow over the entire village, a dark reminder of the dangers of disobedience and the wrath of the unknown forces tied to the mystical liondo.

As the arguments and accusations raged on, the only sound that rose above them was the distant cry of Liusi, still carrying Wekulo's desperate plea across the skies toward Mumbo, where Kasawa would soon hear of the devastating fate that had befallen his children.

vi). An Encounter with the Bukusu Sacred Land

Kasawa was in the middle of crafting a new plough, his hammer striking the red-hot metal with a rhythmic clang, when he heard a distant, melodious song. The sound was faint at first, like a breeze whispering through the leaves, but it was unlike anything he had heard before. He stopped his work, letting the hammer rest on the anvil, and listened more closely.

As he strained to hear, the song grew louder, the voice coming closer and closer. There was something familiar about it, something that tugged at his soul. The words started to form in his mind, though still faint and muddled. Kasawa tried to shake off the distraction, believing his ears were playing tricks on him. He rubbed his ears with his smaller fingers, hoping to clear whatever was obstructing his hearing. But when he removed his fingers, the song only grew more distinct.

The lyrics became clearer, and his heart sank as he recognized his own name being sung by the bird. Then, he heard the word *liondo*, and finally, the most chilling of all—eighteen children. His children! Panic gripped his heart, and without a second thought, he sprang up from his workstation, abandoning his tools. In his haste, he forgot the crucial step of whistling to summon the mysterious ladder that always took him up and down from *Mumbo*.

Kasawa's mind was so clouded with fear and confusion that he nearly slipped off the edge of the high cliffs of Mumbo. Just as he teetered on the brink, the ladder seemed to sense his distress. With a sudden whoosh, it appeared beneath him, lifting him away from danger. But instead of descending the mountain as it usually did, the ladder took him higher, lifting him to the other side of Mumbo. It was as if an unseen force guided it, carrying Kasawa to a place he had never been before.

Kasawa's breath caught in his throat as he found himself standing in a strange, serene realm. The air was thick with a sacred calm, and the land stretched out before him, bathed in an ethereal glow. In the distance, he saw a gathering of figures, their white robes gleaming in the light. As he approached, his heart pounded, both in awe and fear. The closer he got, the more he recognized these figures—*Mukhobe*, the great *Bukusu ancestor* who served as a mediator between the Bukusu people and their god, *Wele Khakaba*.

Beside Mukhobe stood *Mwambu*, the revered ancestor known for his wisdom and bravery, along with *twenty-eight elderly beings*, all dressed in white robes. Each one had an aura of deep knowledge and authority. Kasawa knew he was in the presence of his ancestors—guardians of the Bukusu heritage and tradition.

Trembling with a mixture of reverence and fear, Kasawa fell to his knees and bowed low before the assembly of his forebears. "I greet you, my honored ancestors," he said, his voice quivering. "I am humbled to stand before you today."

Mukhobe, with his wise, ancient eyes, looked down upon Kasawa. "Rise, Kasawa," he said, his voice deep and resonant, carrying the weight of centuries. "You have been brought here because the cries of your heart have reached us. Speak and tell us what troubles you."

Kasawa raised slowly, his face lined with worry and sorrow. "My ancestors," he began, "I have planted a strange *liondo* in my garden, a fruit whose seeds I brought from my secret place here in Mumbo. I believed it would be a blessing for my family, to use for medicine and nourishment. But while I was away, something terrible happened. My children, eighteen of them, have died after eating this cursed fruit. I do not know how or why, but I fear I have brought a great evil upon my family." His voice broke, and his eyes filled with tears.

The elders murmured amongst themselves, and Mukhobe nodded thoughtfully. "Indeed, Kasawa, the *liondo* you brought from Mumbo is no ordinary fruit," he said solemnly. "It is a sacred fruit, meant only for the gods and spirits of this realm. To bring it to the mortal world is to invite disaster, for it carries with it the power of life and death. Your children, innocent as they were, have fallen victim to this curse."

Kasawa's knees trembled, and he clasped his hands together in desperation. "Please, my ancestors, I beg you, show me mercy! Is there any way to save my children? I did not mean to defy the divine order. I only sought to provide for my family."

Machula, one of the wise elders, stepped forward. "There may be a way," he said his voice softer but filled with authority. "The souls of your children are not yet lost to us. They linger at the threshold between the living and the spirit world, caught in the grip of the *liondo's* curse. But to break this course, you must undertake a journey—a journey that will test your faith, your courage, and your love for your family."

Mwambu added, "You must appease *Wele Khakaba* with the smell of a sacred leaf to call back the souls of your children from the brink of the spirit world. Kasawa nodded, his face set with determination. "I will do whatever it takes, my ancestors.

vii). The Sacred Leaf and the Redemption of Bukusu Land

Kasawa stood in front of his ancestors, his heart heavy with the weight of their words. He had not meant to bring harm to his family, but now he understood the gravity of his mistake. The *liondo* he had taken from *Mumbo* was not just any plant—it was a sacred one, hidden away by *Wele Khakaba,* the Bukusu god, from the mortal world. The powerful knowledge hit him like a blow.

Mukhobe looked at Kasawa with eyes that seemed to pierce through his very soul. "Kasawa," he said in a voice filled with both wisdom and authority, "you have transgressed the boundary between the mortal and the divine. The liondo you brought back to your home was never meant for the eyes, or the hands, of humans. It is a secret plant, guarded by *Wele Khakaba* himself, and it carries within it both the gift of life and the curse of death."

Kasawa bowed his head in shame. "I did not know, Mukhobe. I was blinded by my desire to provide for my family. I thought I was bringing back something that would help them, not harm them."

Mukhobe nodded, acknowledging Kasawa's remorse. "Your intentions were not malicious, and for that reason, Wele Khakaba has shown mercy upon you. But you must understand that the world of the gods and the world of men are not meant to intertwine in such ways. There are plants; there are secrets that are not meant for human hands."

With a slow, deliberate step, Mukhobe moved a few feet away from the assembly of ancestors. The ground seemed to shimmer beneath his feet, and he reached down to pluck a leaf from another mysterious plant that grew in the sacred soil of Mumbo. The plant's leaves were a deep emerald green, glistening as if they were kissed by morning dew, even in the ethereal light of this sacred place.

Mukhobe returned to Kasawa and handed him the leaf with great care. "Take this, Kasawa," he said. "This leaf is from the sacred garden of the gods and the spirits of this realm. With it, you must prepare a small pot of soup, mixed with salt, and nothing more. When you return home, you must put a single drop of this soup into each child's mouth. This will bring them back from the edge of the spirit world, back to the realm of the living."

Kasawa's eyes filled with tears, a mix of relief and gratitude. "Thank you, *Mukhobe*. Thank you, great ancestors. I will do as you instruct. I will not let your wisdom be in vain."

But *Mukhobe's* face remained stern. "Remember this, Kasawa," he warned. "This mercy comes with a condition. You must never again take any plant from the realm of the gods and bring it into the world of men. These plants are not meant for mortals; their power can cause great havoc if misused. As for the *liondo* in your garden, you must destroy it. Uproot the plant and burn it to ash. Only then will the curse be lifted fully from your home."

Kasawa nodded solemnly, understanding the weight of his task. "I will, *Mukhobe*. I will destroy the *liondo* plant and ensure that no trace of it remains in my garden."

Mukhobe's gaze softened and he placed a reassuring hand on Kasawa's shoulder. "Go now, Kasawa. Time is of the essence. Your children's souls are lingering at the threshold, waiting for your return."

With a deep breath and newfound determination, Kasawa bowed to his ancestors one last time. He turned and ran back to the mysterious ladder, clutching the magic leaf tightly in his hand. The ladder sensed his urgency and swiftly descended, carrying him down the cliffs of Mumbo and back to the familiar earth of the Cherenganyi Hills.

Kasawa's feet barely touched the ground when he broke into a sprint, his heart pounding with both fear and hope. The journey back to his village felt like an eternity, every step echoing his desperation to reach his home before it was too late.

After bidding farewell to his ancestors, Kasawa felt a sudden whoosh, and in the blink of an eye, he was back in his village, standing at the rear of his house. There was no time to waste. His heart was pounding, and he could hear the muffled cries and murmurs from the front of his home, where the crows had gathered in disbelief. Kasawa knew he needed to act swiftly to save his children.

Without pausing to catch his breath or answer the bewildered looks of his neighbors, he rushed straight into the kitchen. His hands worked with the precision of a master blacksmith, preparing the soup exactly as Mukhobe had instructed. The magic leaf simmered gently in the water, its potent scent mingling with the smoke from the fire. He added just a pinch of salt, stirring it carefully as he prayed silently to Wele Khakaba.

With the bowl of the sacred soup ready, Kasawa hurried to where the lifeless bodies of his children lay, still and cold. The sight of them, his precious children lying there, broke his heart, but he steeled himself. He could not allow grief to overwhelm him; there was work to be done.

One by one, he cradled each child in his arms and gently dropped a single drop of the soup into their mouths. For a moment, nothing happened. The crows and villagers watching held their breath, and the world seemed to pause. But then, with a soft gasp, the first child, Namikoye, took a deep breath. Color returned to her cheeks, and her eyes fluttered open. The crowd gasped, and tears flowed freely.

Kasawa continued his sacred task, moving from child to child. Netondo, Nanjakho, Namakanda, and each of the others began to stir, life returning to their bodies. In no time, all eighteen of his children were awake, breathing, and looking around with dazed eyes. Wekulo, who had not partaken of the liondo, burst into tears of relief, hugging his siblings tightly.

The children, still trembling from their ordeal, looked at their parents with remorseful eyes. "We are sorry, Baba, Mama," Namikoye spoke first, her voice filled with regret and fear. "We disobeyed you, and we paid the price. We promise never to disrespect you again."

Their heartfelt apologies echoed among the crowd. The villagers watched in awe, whispering prayers of thanks to Wele Khakaba and expressing their astonishment at the miracle they had just witnessed. Kasawa embraced his children, his heart full, and forgave them for their disobedience, knowing they had learned a lesson that would remain with them forever.

With his children restored to life, Kasawa turned his attention to the cursed plant that had caused all this misery. He marched into the garden, where the liondo plant stood—its large, smooth fruit was the source of their ordeal. Without hesitation, he grasped the thick stem and uprooted the entire plant. The crowd watched in silence as he dragged it to the center of the yard, piled it high with dry sticks, and set it ablaze. The flames rose high, crackling and consuming the plant until it was nothing but ashes.

The smoke billowed into the sky, carrying with it the curse that had lingered over his household. Kasawa sighed with relief, knowing he had fulfilled his promise to Mukhobe and ensured the safety of his family.

News of Kasawa's ordeal and the miraculous revival of his children spread rapidly throughout the village of Eluhyia and beyond. The whispers reached the ears of the community chief, a wise elder who commanded great respect among the Bukusu people. Intrigued and moved by the story, the chief sent a summons for Kasawa to come to his court.

When Kasawa arrived, he stood before the great chief and humbly recounted everything that had transpired—from the forbidden fruit of Mumbo to his encounter with Mukhobe and the revival of his children. The chief listened attentively, nodding thoughtfully as Kasawa spoke.

"Indeed," the chief said after a long silence, "Wele Khakaba watches over his people, and through Mukhobe, we are granted mercy and guidance. Kasawa, your story is a powerful reminder of the divine's presence among us and the need to respect the boundaries set by the gods."

The chief then stood, addressing the gathered elders and villagers. "From this day forward," he proclaimed, "let it be known that all Bukusu people shall honor and pray to Wele Khakaba through our mediator, Mukhobe. He is our guardian angel, and it is through his wisdom and guidance that we are kept safe. Let us teach our children to respect the laws of the gods and to cherish the gifts they bestow upon us."

The villagers cheered, raising their hands to the sky in praise of Wele Khakaba and in gratitude for Kasawa's courage and wisdom. The village of Eluhyia flourished, and the story of Kasawa and the mysterious pumpkin fruit became a legend, passed down from generation to generation, a tale of respect, redemption, and the ever-watchful eyes of the gods.

And so, life in the village returned to normal, but with a renewed sense of reverence for the mysteries of the world around them, and a deep respect for the unseen forces that governed their lives.

<u>**End**</u>

Gûkumbacwo in Muiruri's Farm

i).Gaturu the Lazy Squirrel

Once upon a time, in a lively village of Matunda, in Gātanga, Kenya lived a lazy squirrel named Gaturu. This animal had a big appetite and an even bigger love for lounging under shady trees. He loved to munch on nuts, fruits, and anything tasty he could find, but he disliked working for them. Most of the other animals in the village were hard working and spent their days planting, farming, and gathering food. But not Gaturu; he would rather sleep all day!

One day, his old grandmother called him and said, "Gaturu, you are old enough now to help with the farm work. Here, take these groundnut seeds and go plant them in our farm. When they grow, we'll have plenty of groundnuts to eat all year long."

Gaturu reluctantly took the seeds and lazily made his way to the family farm. As he walked, his belly began to rumble. "Oh, I'm so hungry," he muttered to himself. "These groundnut seeds look so delicious." Instead of planting them, the lazy squirrel started eating the seeds, one by one, until there were none left!

With a full belly, he rolled around in the soil for a while to make it look like he had been working hard. Then, he trudged back home and pretended to be exhausted. "Oh, Grandmother," he said, panting and wiping his brow, "I have worked so hard today planting the groundnuts! I'm so tired."

His grandmother, not suspecting his trick, was pleased. She prepared him a big meal to reward him for his "hard work." Gaturu grinned from ear to ear as he gobbled up the food. Days turned into weeks, and weeks turned into months. The lazy squirrel continued to pretend that he was tending to the groundnut farm.

One day, his grandmother told him, "The groundnuts must be ready for weeding by now. Go and weed them, and soon we'll have a bountiful harvest." Gaturu had no choice but to go to the farm. But when he got there, he found nothing but bare soil—there were no groundnuts because he had eaten them all!

To keep up his act, he rolled around in the soil again, dusted himself with dirt, and came back home pretending to be tired. "The groundnuts are growing so well, Grandmother!" he said, trying to sound convincing.

The next day, while wandering lazily around the village, Gaturu stumbled upon Muiruri's thriving firm. His eyes widened with delight when he saw rows upon rows of groundnut plants thriving under the sun. "Oh, what a magnificent sight!" he whispered to himself. "Look at all those delicious groundnuts. If only they were mine..."

The greedy squirrel's mind began to churn with a sneaky plan. "When these groundnuts are ready, I will come back at night and harvest them all. No one will ever know!" he thought.

ii). Gaturu's Love for Free Things

When Muiruri's groundnuts were finally ready for harvest, Gaturu decided it was time to put his sneaky plan into action. One dark night, when everyone was asleep and the moon hid behind thick clouds, Gaturu crept quietly into Muiruri's farm. His little paws moved swiftly, and his eyes darted around, making sure no one was watching. He worked quickly, harvesting one section of the lush, green groundnuts. He bundled them up and carried them back home to his grandmother.

When he reached home, he woke his grandmother, who was surprised to see so many groundnuts. "Oh, Gaturu!" she exclaimed, "You have done marvelous work this season! I didn't think we would have such a bountiful harvest!" The old grandmother was pleased and didn't suspect a thing.

The following night, Gaturu, filled with greed, decided to raid Muiruri's farm again. He snuck back into the farm, where the groundnuts were still glistening with dew. This time, he harvested the remaining section. With his loot in hand, he hurried back home under the cover of darkness, his heart racing with excitement.

Meanwhile, Muiruri, a hardworking man known for his patience and wisdom, decided to check on his farm the next morning. As he approached the field, his heart sank. The sight before him was not pleasing at all! "Oh no!" he exclaimed, "Who could have stolen my groundnuts?" His beautiful groundnut farm was almost bare, with only a few plants left untouched.

Muiruri knew he had to think quickly. He went back home, sat on his wooden stool under the big baobab tree, and began to plan on what to do. "The thief will surely come back to finish off the rest," he thought. "I must come up with a clever plan to catch him in the act!"

iii). Confrontation in Muiruri's Farm

On the third night, Gaturu, filled with confidence from his previous raids, crept back to Muiruri's farm under the cover of darkness. His eyes gleamed with greed as he began to harvest the remaining section of the groundnuts, humming to himself about the feast he would have.

Suddenly, in the dim moonlight, Gaturu noticed a strange figure standing among the groundnut plants. It looked somewhat like him, but its presence felt off. Annoyed, he said, "How dare you refuse to greet me? Don't you know who I am?" The figure, silent and still, made no reply.

Feeling insulted and angry, Gaturu yelled, "I will teach you a lesson of your life!" He rushed toward the figure and slapped it hard on the chest. But to his surprise, his hand got stuck to the figure. He pulled and pulled, but it wouldn't budge.

"You think you can hold my hand and get away with it? I will show you!" Gaturu shouted in fury. He slapped the figure with his other hand, but that one also got stuck! Now growing frantic, he kicked it with one foot, and then the other, only to find both his feet stuck as well.

With panic setting in, he shouted, "You have crossed the line now! I'll use my head to headbutt you into pieces!" But when Gaturu rammed his head against the figure, it too got stuck. There he was, completely trapped and unable to move, stuck fast to a unique scarecrow that Muiruri had cleverly set up in his farm. The kimakia ndurû, the scarecrow was coated in a sticky sap from the fig tree, making it nearly impossible for anything that touched it to get free.

The night grew darker, and Gaturu realized he had been outsmarted. He began to panic, knowing he had no way to escape. As dawn began to break, he could only hope for a miracle or brace himself for the consequences of his actions when Muiruri returned to his farm.

The following morning, Muiruri, accompanied by his son, Muturi, returned to the farm to check on the scarecrow trap. To their surprise, they found Gaturu, the lazy squirrel stuck tightly to *kimakia ndurû*, wiggling and struggling but unable to break free. "So, it's you, Gaturu (the thief)!" Muiruri exclaimed, recognizing the squirrel that had been stealing his groundnuts.

With a firm grip, Muiruri bundled up Gaturu and took him home. He needed to decide what to do with this troublesome thief. After some thought, he handed Gaturu, the squirrel over to his wife. "Prepare a delicious meal for us tonight," he told her, thinking they would feast on the naughty squirrel that had caused him so much trouble.

The wife, eager to please her husband, began gathering the ingredients to cook Gaturu. While she was busy preparing, Gaturu, who had a sly grin on his face, said to her, "If you want your husband and son to truly enjoy my meat, do not cut me into pieces. Just immerse me in a pot of water as I am, and do not cover the lid."

The wife, trusting the squirrel's words, followed his instructions. She placed Gaturu in a pot of water and left the kitchen to get some salt from the large house. As soon as she left, Muturi, Muiruri's son, entered the kitchen to add more firewood to the fire.

The cunning Gaturu peeked out of the pot and, with a cheeky grin, mocked Muturi, "Thank you for adding the firewood, but you'll never taste a bite of me!" Before Muturi could react, Gaturu jumped out of the pot, his fur still wet but unharmed. With a swift leap, he dashed out of the kitchen door and disappeared into the nearby bushes, free once again.

Gaturu left Muiruri's family in utter disbelief that evening. The delicious meal they had anticipated was nowhere to be seen, and they were left with an empty pot and a lesson learned about the squirrel's cunning nature. Though Gaturu managed to escape death, the confrontation with Muiruri and his family had serious consequences.

Gaturu began hiding deep into the bushes, fearing that Muiruri, his family members or human relatives would harm him. His greed and trickery had brought him close to danger, and he knew better than to return to Muiruri's farm again. To this day, Gaturu remains in hiding, wary of the humans he once tried to outwit, forever known as the lazy squirrel that couldn't resist a good trick but learned the hard way to be cautious of his actions.

WASIKE

<u>End.</u>

Naswa and the Talking Pumpkin Fruit

WASIKE

In a small village nestled on the edge of the Sub-Saharan Africa, there lived a young girl named Naswa. She was known throughout Chekulo village for her kindness and a heart that could rival the sun in warmth. Her family was poor, and her father, Elder Walubengo, had recently fallen ill, leaving Naswa to care for her younger siblings: Mukhwana, Mulongo, Wesakulila and Khaemba. Despite her struggles, she never lost her smile, and her spirit remained unbroken.

One scorching afternoon, as the village baked under the relentless sun, Naswa decided to go fetch water from the distant stream. The journey was long and exhausting, but she walked with determination, humming a soft melody her mother used to sing.

Along the way, she passed by a wild pumpkin plant with roots thick and gnarled like the hands of an elder. This was no ordinary plant because it had produced a huge pumpkin fruit that could talk. Although many considered this plant an ancient fairy tales, it had been around but invisible to many generations. As such, the village's rich history was part and parcel of this magical pumpkin plant. Its decision to reveal itself to Naswa means she had something special.

As she sat there, lost in thought, she heard a deep, rumbling voice. "Why are you troubled, young one?" Startled, Naswa looked around and realized it was the huge pumpkin fruit speaking to her.

"I am not troubled," she replied softly. "I am just worried about my father. He is very sick, and I don't know how to help him."

Sensing the sincerity in her voice, the magic fruit said, "I have watched over this land for centuries, and I know the secrets of the earth. There is a rare flower called the Moon's Tear, which blooms once a year under the light of the full moon. It grows on the highest peak of Cherenganyi hills, far from here. Its petals can heal any ailment, but the journey is perilous, and many who have sought it never returned."

Naswa's heart pounded with hope and fear. She knew the journey would be dangerous, but the thought of her father suffering was unbearable. Without hesitation, she thanked the pumpkin fruit and set off toward Cherenganyi hills.

The path was arduous; she crossed vast plains, waded through muddy swamps, and climbed steep hills. She encountered wild animals and had to navigate treacherous terrain. But through it all, she kept her father's smile in her heart, fueling her courage.

After several days, Naswa finally reached the base of Cherenganyi hills. The peak seemed to touch the sky, and her body was exhausted, but she pressed on. As she climbed, the air grew thin, and her legs trembled with every step. She could hear the whispers of spirits in the wind, warning her to turn back, but she refused.

Finally, on the night of the full moon, Naswa reached the summit. There, bathed in the soft silver light, was the Moon's Tear, a delicate flower with petals that shimmered like diamonds. Tears welled in her eyes, and with trembling hands, she plucked the flower, thanking the ancestors for guiding her.

But as she turned to leave, the mountain began to shake, and a fierce wind blew. Out of the shadows emerged a Giant Serpent named *Endemu,* its scales glistening like obsidian. It was the guardian of the Moon's Tear, and it hissed with fury, "Who dares steal from me?"

Naswa, though terrified, stood her ground. "I am Naswa, and I took this flower to save my father. I mean no harm to you or this land."

Endemu's eyes glowed like embers. "Many have come before you with greed in their hearts, but I sense something different in you—a love that is pure and selfless."

Seeing her bravery and honesty, the Serpent's anger softened. "You may leave with the flower," it said, "but remember, the greatest magic in this world is not found in rare flowers or spells but in the love and sacrifice we show for one another."

Naswa bowed with gratitude and descended the hills' terrains, her heart light despite her weary body. She returned to her village, where she used the petals of the Moon's Tear to brew a potion for her father. As he drank it, color returned to his cheeks, and his strength was restored.

The inhabitants of Chekulo celebrated Naswa's courage and love, and from that day on, they revered the Talking pumpkin fruit and Endemu, understanding that true magic lives in the heart that beats with love and selflessness.

End

The Cry of the Widow's Son

In a remote village nestled between rolling hills and dense forests, there lived a young boy named Wakonambi and his mother, Nekesa, a widow. Wakonambi was a bright-eyed child with a heart full of dreams and a spirit as free as the wind. He and his mother were inseparable; she was his world, and he was hers.

Nekesa was a farmer, toiling day and night to provide for her son after the tragic loss of her husband to a mysterious illness. Despite the hardships, she always wore a warm smile and filled their small mud house with songs of love and hope. Wakonambi would sit by the doorway, listening to her sing, his heart swelling with love for the woman who gave everything for him.

One fateful year, a severe drought struck the village. The fields dried up, and the riverbeds turned to dust. Food became scarce, and hunger spread like a shadow over the land. Nekesa's farm, which was their only means of survival, yielded nothing but parched soil and dying crops. Yet, every night, she would still sing to Wakonambi, her voice trembling with both weariness and courage.

One day, Nekesa fell gravely ill. The drought had drained her body and spirit. She grew weaker with each passing day, her songs fading to whispers. Wakonambi, desperate to save his mother, remembered an old tale she had told him about the *River of Life*, a mystical stream hidden deep within the *Forest of Whispers*. Its waters, she had said, were said to have the power to heal any illness and bring life to the dying.

Determined to save his mother, Wakonambi set off on a journey to find the River of Life. He walked for days, through thorny bushes and dense trees, his small feet bleeding and his body aching with hunger. But the thought of his mother's gentle face kept him going. As he ventured deeper into the Forest of Whispers, he encountered spirits and creatures that tried to dissuade him from continuing.

"Turn back, little boy," they warned. "The path ahead is full of danger and sorrow."

With tears in his eyes and love in his heart, Wakonambi pressed on. "I must save my mother," he whispered.

Finally, after many days of wandering, Wakonambi reached a clearing where he saw a glimmering stream—the River of Life. The water sparkled like diamonds under the moonlight, and his heart leaped with hope. He knelt by the riverbank, cupping the water in his hands, ready to carry it back to his mother.

But as he turned to leave, an ancient spirit emerged from the river, its form shimmering and translucent. "Child," the spirit spoke in a voice that seemed to echo through time, "you seek to save your mother, but know this: the River of Life demands a sacrifice. For every drop you take, a piece of your own life will be given in return."

Wakonambi's heart sank. He was just a child, full of dreams of growing up, of one day becoming a man his mother could be proud of. But as he looked into the clear waters of the river, he saw the reflection of his mother's face, pale and fragile. The choice was clear.

With trembling hands, Wakonambi filled his small gourd with the enchanted water, feeling his own strength begin to fade with every drop. His legs grew weak, his vision blurred, but he clutched the gourd to his chest and began the journey back home.

The forest seemed darker and more menacing on his return, and his body grew colder with every step. But he kept moving, driven by the thought of his mother's smile. After what felt like an eternity, Wakonambi stumbled back into his village, barely able to stand. His breath was shallow, his body weak, but he managed to reach their small mud house.

Inside, he found his mother, laying still, her breathing faint. With the last of his strength, Wakonambi brought the gourd to her lips and let the healing waters flow. Slowly, color returned to Nekesa cheeks, and her eyes fluttered open. She saw her son before her, his face pale, his eyes filled with tears.

"Wakonambi, what have you done?" she whispered, her voice breaking.

"I... I brought you the River of Life, Mama," he replied weakly, his voice trembling. "I couldn't let you leave me."

Realizing what he had sacrificed Nekesa's heart shattered. She gathered him in her arms, tears streaming down her face. "No, my son, my precious boy... You were my life."

As the last breath left Wakonambi's body, the village, now awakened, stood in silence, witnessing the purest act of love they had ever seen. Nekesa's wails pierced the night, echoing through the hills and forests. The drought ended the next day, and the rains returned, as if the heavens themselves mourned the loss of a brave soul.

Nekesa never sang again, but the villagers sang for her, a song of Wakonambi, the boy who gave everything for his mother. His story became a legend, passed down through generations, a reminder that the deepest love is one that knows no bounds—even beyond life itself.

And so, Wakonambi's spirit lived on in the hearts of those who heard his tale, a testament to the power of love and sacrifice.